W9-DIG-767

MEMOIRS OF A
BROKENHEARTED GIRL

REIGN LEE

Copyright © 2020 by Reign Lee

All rights reserved.

No part of this book may be reproduced in any form or by any electronic or mechanical means, including information storage and retrieval systems, without written permission from the author, except for the use of brief quotations in a book review.

ACKNOWLEDGMENTS

First, I want to thank God, for everything that he has done for me. The things that he has allowed to help me grow into a better person and for the things that he has protected me from. I also want to thank my family and friends, you know who you are, for always being an ear and understanding that what I aspire to become requires them to share me a lot with the computer. Next, I want to thank my wonderful publisher, Nikki Brown, for all her support, advice, and gentle nudges that makes me challenge myself as a writer. Last, but not least my readers. I appreciate your comments and feedback more than you know. Thank you for choosing to read any of my books. I hope you continue to keep me in your catalogs as we take this journey together.

SYNOPSIS

As a girl growing up, it was made known that my whole existence was predicated on me being my parent's meal ticket, and when that plan bombed, I was left with a rough life ahead. I lived on my own at an early age and learned how to grow up fast, especially from these three men. Will, Bronte, and Cortez.

My first true love gave me my very first everything, and just as easily took it away, and strangely enough, I still cared for him. Then the next man, whom my world revolved around, gave me everything that I never wanted, yet I took it, along with so much more that I cannot get rid of even if I tried. Then there was always that one that you liked a little but used. Yeah, him! He was around too, but that mentality tends to bite you in the butt sooner or later, and let's just say I got bit... hard!

All three men ultimately had an impact on my life, one way or another, and changed it in ways I couldn't have imagined. Forever! Come inside and follow my journey and see how things transpired for me in Memoirs of a Broken-Hearted Girl.

1

SEPTEMBER 4, 2005

Never been one to believe in celebrating anything but for some reason today, I was summoned to do so. Bronte's voice came booming through the air from downstairs startling me, out of my sleep. I furiously sat up with both hands digging in the bed wondering what the fuck was he hollering about.

"Babe! Yo, Gold! I gotta run out for a bit. Get dressed up for me tonight please. I got something planned for us later."

"What!"

Then I heard the front door slam. He'd never asked that of me in the seven years we'd been together. But I did as he asked and got dressed up later that night. I hadn't heard from Bronte since he left out in the morning. That wasn't unusual, but what was, was his request. I figured, maybe he was out still working on what he had planned for us, so I didn't press the issue and bug him, until it was after eight o'clock at night. I tried to call him, but he didn't answer, so I called him again, putting it on speaker when he finally picked up.

"What's up?"

"The first time I called wasn't good enough after I've been sitting here all dolled the fuck up for you?" I sassed, shaking my head as I spoke.

"I'm conducting business."

"Bronte, when are you coming home? I thought you had something planned for us."

"I ran into a lil' problem, but I'll be home as soon as I can."

"What problem, Bronte! You asked me to get dressed up, when you know I couldn't care less about doing shit on my birthday, and then you say some bullshit like this to me."

He had my blood boiling like lava.

"I know, babe. I'm sorry. You know I have no way of knowing sometimes how my day's gonna be. I had to tend to something unexpect— who... who dat talking in the background?"

"It's the television."

"You bet' not have a nigga up in there."

"And what if it was... what could you do?" I had to fuck with him since he pissed me off. "You're not even here," I reiterated, giving the phone an evil eye.

"Man, Golden, don't play with me like dat."

"You know good and well it ain't no nigga up in here, so stop trippin'. You supposed to be here."

"Man, don't get fucked up!" he yelled, riled up.

"You'd have to be around enough first."

"Yeah, keep talking shit. I gotta go. I'll see you tonight. I love you."

"Yeah, whatever, Bronte."

Frustration was what I felt at that moment. Not love, so he could've saved that shit.

"Why I don't hear you saying it back?"

"You know I love you."

Although, I was starting to question it.

"Say it."

"I just did."

"Say my name when you say it."

I looked at my phone and rolled my eyes at his request.

"I love you, Bronte," I muttered sweetly. "You happy?"

"Yo' ass play too fuckin' much. You better love me," he ordered. "I'll call you when I'm on my way home."

I threw my phone on the couch with so much aggression. He knew how I felt about all holidays, and I ain't give no fucks about dressing up for those occasions, not even my birthday. Especially my birthday, knowing my whole existence was one big joke anyway, starting from conception.

You know my parents named me Golden because I was supposed to be their *golden* ticket? When I say that, I mean my mother told me she only birthed me because she was getting paid to do so. Ain't that some shit! Turned out, the son of a bitch that was supposed to pay the balance on my date of birth, skipped the fuck out after I was brought home from the hospital. I wasn't so *golden* anymore.

Hell, I became aware of that real quick as I got older. There was no need to get excited about shit. Nothing changed in our house except the days of the week. Halloween surely wasn't no treat. Thanksgiving didn't put more food on our table, and Christmas definitely didn't bring me toys.

But back to the reason I hated my birthday the most. For one, instead of me being celebrated, my parents celebrated that I was another birthday closer to being put out. I knew the moment I could understand the word *departure,* that was what I had to do at eighteen. How wonderful were they.

They would play loud music and celebrate with a big bottle of vodka. Drank it straight. Danced until one of them got pissed off, flipped off, and then told the fuck off for drinking the last drop of booze, then fought like two drunk fools. If I had somewhere else to go before eighteen, I would've been departed.

I watched my mother endure years of physical abuse from my father, since she wouldn't back down, and vice versa, until she killed him when I was fourteen. I saw her shoot him right in the head on my birthday, the second reason why I hated it. All I had, even though they weren't shit, was taken away from me that day. He died instantly, and she was sent to prison.

I ended up living with a friend of hers named Anniqua, or Ms. Nique as I had to call her. I hated that bitch. She treated me like I was a damn slave. Made me wash the walls, the baseboards, do all the laundry, and clean the bathroom every Saturday. The kitchen was my responsibility daily. She didn't lift a foot nor finger, but I lifted my hands and bashed her in her fuckin' face when I was sixteen because she tried to make me clean up a shit-filled bathroom with throw up everywhere that her drunk ass lover left sitting all night.

By then, I had a boyfriend, and he talked his mom into letting me stay with them. That lasted until I got pregnant a year later after graduation when I was seventeen. I got too comfortable, I guess, because we were screwing like jack rabbits and nothing never happened, until it did.

Will, my man at the time, paid for me to get an abortion. I wanted that baby, but his mother talked me out of it, saying we ain't have shit to offer it and no place to raise it. Will didn't want it anyway. At that point, he didn't want me either. I had to go, and my exit wasn't so pretty.

Later, I realized why he was so quick to want the abortion and so easily ready to dismiss me out of his life. He was already fuckin' 'round with another bitch, telling her I was his best friend living with them. That right there filled me with even more resentment and animosity, which made me go back to his part of town after I'd left it and fuck his whole world up like he did mine.

For two nights, I slept on the subway train in *Nerk Circle,* where my ex was from. A girlfriend of mine that I knew from school named Giselle, saw me asleep the second night with my things and spoke with her family about me staying with them. That was how I met her brother Cortez. He was visiting home from college at that time during his junior year. Cortez was a looker. My skin was rich with color like cocoa and I always seemed to attract light skinned dudes.

He flirted with me every chance he could get, but I never gave him the time of day until we bumped into each other six years later. I was twenty-three by then; he was twenty-six. I was walking out of *Grand Tree Heights,* a home share I was staying at, renting a room. As I was rushing out the door, he was coming in, and I literally bumped right into him, knocking his supplies out his hands.

"Oh shit! I'm so sorry!" I expressed sincerely.

I watched him as he bent down to pick up his things.

"No, it's okay," he said before he stood up and I got to see his face.

"Cortez?"

His smile, so warm and inviting, spread across his face so fast like a wildfire.

"Golden? Damn, girl! Look at you." I wasn't the same either. He dropped his things again and grabbed me, wrapping me in his arms and lifting me off my feet. I looked down into his coffee brown eyes that showcased his wispy lashes. He had a beard now, neatly groomed close to his face, that traveled around his full lips. He wasn't that scrawny boy that I used to know. No, sir! He grew into one hell of a man, and damn did it show. Slowly, those cut arms put me down. Everything on him was so muscular and firm as my body slid down his, our clothes causing friction, making my body pause every now and then until my feet finally touched the floor. "What are you doing here?" he finally eased out.

"Me? I live here." I stared at him, stunned. But the feeling was mutual. His eyes were glued to me, absorbing every bit of me like a wet sponge as he stared at me. It had been so long; I just never expected to see him and this transformation. He looked so fine and handsome. Someone opened the door, which made Cortez pick his things back up so they wouldn't be in the way. Afterwards, he stood beside me as the lady passed, eyeing him hard with a telling smile on her face. "Are you working somewhere in here?" I curiously asked as my eyes continued to smile at him.

"I'm just here to see the owner."

"For? She in trouble?"

He smiled.

"No, she's not in trouble."

"Shouldn't you be solving crime, or are you a psychologist of some sort now?"

He sighed and shook his head as his eyes widened with an emptiness to them.

"What I should be doing and want to be doing don't always go hand and hand, but..."

"But what?"

I knew I had to go because I was running late as it was for an appointment, but I was curious about Cortez.

"But just know I can arrest you and still fuck with ya mind," he confessed.

In my head, I was thinking, *arrest me already, because my mind is already fucked.* Just seeing him made me realize how much I missed him, with his flirting ass. We fooled around for a while after that, which I was fine with, but eventually, he wanted more. I wasn't ready for that. I was just enjoying getting my ass waxed and back blown out every now and then. Cortez was a great guy, but in the back of my mind, I was always afraid of him hurting me. He deserved so much better, and I knew he'd find it and leave, so I took that opportunity and bailed... called it quits.

I hadn't made the best choices in life or been dealt the best hand, but I knew getting that abortion was one that changed me and still stung. It made me realize I had to do what was best for me, right or wrong. I was learning the hard way that no one else would have my best interest but me. With Cortez, I was only doing what was best for me. Here I was, seven years in with Bronte, and I wondered from time to time, if I would've made a different choice, what would my life with Cortez have looked like in the long run. Especially when shit like this happened.

I'd dealt with a lot when it came to Bronte. Mostly because I believed he was who I deserved. I knew he loved me and meant well. I just didn't know if it was enough anymore. I never thought I'd feel this way, but I was tired. I was tired of not being enough for him, and after he did this to me today, knowing how much I hated my birthday, really let me know I had a decision to finally make.

I NOTICED it was after three in the morning, and he came in and jumped right in the shower. Next, he laid beside me and wrapped his arms around me like everything was okay. I guess I'd allowed this to go on for too long, but I couldn't put up with this anymore. I flung his arm off me, sat up, and turned on the light.

"Who'd you fuck tonight, Bronte, besides fucking me over?" I griped as I shoved him.

"What? What the fuck you talking 'bout, girl, damn! I'm just getting done. Turn that light out and lay ya ass back down."

"Not until we talk," I demanded as I looked over at his sorry ass. "Who'd you fuck, Bronte?" I asked an octave higher since he hadn't answered me yet.

"Golden, baby, lay ya ass down... I'm tired. Let's go to sleep." I pushed him over to his side of the bed away from me. His body was relaxed too, which made it easy for me. "Yo, what you doing?" He huffed.

"Matter of fact, you can have this bed to yourself. I'm going in the other room."

As soon as I got up, Bronte grabbed my arm.

"Where the fuck you think you going?"

"I'm not sleeping in here with you tonight, or any other night for that matter. I'm leaving you, Bronte. I'm tired of ya shit!"

Bronte was laying in the bed, still holding my arm as I was standing. He looked up at me with his face laced with annoyance.

"Why you think I'm out fucking somebody all the time? Is that why you really mad, or because I didn't come back in time to take you out for ya birthday."

"Fuck a birthday! You smelled of sex when you came in here with ya nasty ass, but had me fix myself up. For what! I'm so stupid!" I stressed. "You think I don't know your pattern by now," I said, shaking my head. "But I do! I've been putting up with your cheating ass for seven years too long. It's like it's become a normalcy that I've accepted. Well, I refuse to accept it anymore. I deserve better than this, Taye, especially from you."

"Oh, you know that now... So what I give you is not good enough anymore? Is that what you're saying?"

"What you give me?" *No he did not say that bullshit to me, I* thought. "What you give me, Taye! Heartache, stress, lies, infidelity, tears—need I run it down anymore?"

Bronte stood up with his jawbones tight and his fists balled and got in my face.

"That's all I fuckin' give you," he fussed as he gripped my arms and shook me. "I don't provide for you? Make sure you have what you need and whatever you want? Huh!"

His big hands clawed my arms tightly.

"Bronte, you're hurting me! Let go!"

"I ain't letting you go nowhere!" I knew I had a slight advantage because his eyes looked red as fuck. High, tired, probably both. He wasn't in the mood for my shit, but he better had got ready. I was finally able to break from his grasp. I headed for the door of the bedroom. Bronte came after me and grabbed me from behind. He lifted me off my feet and threw me on the bed as easily as a pillow. He wasn't as tired as I thought he was. Then he laid his bare chest partially on top of me, practically mushing in my stomach, while pinning my arms. "You don't believe I love you?"

The disturbed look in his eyes certainly didn't show love and match his words.

"Bronte, why are you acting like this? You're scaring me."

"Answer me!" he shouted.

"You do, baby! You do lo-love me."

He started kissing different places on my face as he talked in between.

"I do love you... My love is always gon' be... for you. It ain't going nowhere," he assured while he then stroked my long, wavy hair and looked deep into my eyes. My fear instantly turned to anger, which then gave me false courage with him.

"Show me then! Fuck me right now," I commanded.

Bronte pressed his lips back against mine again, tonguing me down. He aggressively pulled my panties down and took off his boxers. I laid there in my nightshirt, waiting, wanting to see how fast he could get it up. He rubbed his penis against me first and noticed I was dry as the desert. Sex was not on my mind... leaving his ass was, but I needed to know if he was out fucking tonight. I knew his body too well, and this would definitely give me the strength to go.

To my surprise, his continuous rubbing on my clit got him hard in no time and me moist, no matter how much I tried to fight it. He started penetrating me slowly, as he eased it inside, inch by inch. I felt myself getting wetter by the second. Then, once he was in, he pounded it on me like a cleaver hitting meat. Damn he smashed me real good.

"You wanted to be fucked, right," he yelled tormenting me. "Huh, Golden, baby?"

 I spoke through my moans.

"Mmm... ye-yes! Yes! Dammit! Yes!"

His thrusts had me squirting as he drilled all up and through my pussy walls. I hated how he treated me at times, but I loved how he fucked me all the time. I grabbed the sheets as he held on to my legs. I didn't get any tender kisses, no tongue licking, nothing but roughly fucked. Bronte made me cum, and even though my body was at his mercy, he still didn't show mercy on my body. He pulled his manhood out after I came and flipped me over on my stomach.

"Poke dat ass out." I barely could bend, but that didn't stop him. He just got flat on top of me, stuck it in and kept on stroking, talking his shit. "Ya... fat... ass... gon' take... allll this dick."

I was taking it and so much more. He went so crazy with sexing me. I thought he was going to bust right through me. He had my body rocking so hard on the bed the cries that I tried to get out sounded all choppy.

"Je-sus... Bron-taye... damn... bay... bee... uh! Uh!"

Shortly after, Bronte finally came. I laid there, exhausted, trying to catch my breath. Bronte was still on top of me, now lying flat, resting for a minute. I guess my prediction was wrong about him fucking someone tonight. A part of me was relieved. Maybe something really did come up with work. The other was telling me I was believing what I wanted.

Suddenly, Bronte's cell phone went off. I got a sudden rush of strength like the Incredible Hulk and rolled over, which then pushed him off me and allowed me to grab it, since it was on the nightstand. He tried to stop me from getting it, but I got away. As soon as I picked it up, I ran out the room and quickly slammed the door. I desperately needed to see who it was. Bronte quickly put his boxers on and came chasing after me. I peeked real quick and read what appeared. It was some girl named Jackie. I saw him in the distance closing in on me.

"You liar!"

I threw his phone at him as he came toward me to take it. It hit him in his chest.

"Aw! Okay."

Bronte continued to try to catch me as I ran from him and flew down the stairs, stumbling over my feet. I didn't know where I was trying to go. I just knew I needed to get away from him. He ended up catching me as I was headed for the kitchen and we both ended up falling to the floor. Bronte had me pinned down as I was on my stomach.

"I hate you!" I shouted, trying to squirm free. "You don't care about me!"

"How can you say that! I fuckin' love you, girl! You hear me!" he belted in my ear.

"No! I want to feel it and see it by you not cheating on me and treating me like shit. I'm tired of only hearing it!"

"Oh, you wanna feel it, huh! You wanna feel it, Golden?" He pressed himself up against my ass, making me feel him. "My heart only beatin' because you hold a nigga down. You think I wanna lose that?"

"Tell that shit to Jackie! Get off me, punk ass!"

"Fuck Jackie!"

"Yeah! I bet you did fuck her. Didn't you?"

Bronte put his mouth close to my ears.

"It doesn't matter how many other women I fuck. You the only one whose shit mean something to me, and I got ya punk ass alright." I lowered my head and bit Bronte on the arm to get him to move off me. "Ahh! Shit!" he spat. He grabbed that spot real quick. I tried to crawl from under him and get up, but he grabbed my hips and stopped me in motion. I quickly turned over on my back and tried to kick him. "Fuck's wrong witchu? You think you can fight me now? Huh, Golden!"

"Won't you just leave me alone, Bronte! It's over! I'm sick of ya cheating ass!"

"It ain't over till I say it's the fuck over. You ain't goin' no fuckin' where. I told you that shit already."

I had to show him that I wasn't playing with him anymore. I looked him straight in the eyes and lied.

"That's why I fucked another guy. Now what you gotta say?"

Bronte pressed his arm up against my throat. His forehead wrinkled, and his eyes grew slim.

"What the fuck you say to me?"

I was left gasping for air.

"I... I can't... breathe..."

He moved his arm but still had me in his grasp. I was breathing hard, trying to calm myself, with part of me afraid to repeat it and the other not giving a fuck.

"That's right, Bronte. I went and had sex with someone else too."

"You lying! I know another nigga ain't been in my shit. I molded this pussy," he boasted.

"Move!" I squirmed aggressively, trying to get him off me. His chocolate six-foot stature didn't budge. He squeezed my shoulders, trying to keep me from fighting him.

"Fuck no! You gave another nigga my pussy?"

I was scared. I didn't know if I should keep up with this lie or not, but I wanted him to feel the pain that I was feeling. I never cheated on Bronte, even with all the shit he'd put me through. I truly loved this motherfucka, but I went ahead and looked him in the eyes with a straight face.

"Yes!"

Bronte's fist came in the direction of my face and made me flinch as he got close. I thought he was going to punch me, but he didn't. He started laughing.

"I know you lying to me. That was a nice try doe." He got in my face. "You fix ya lips to say some shit like that to me again, you ain't gon' have no fuckin' lips fo'real."

"Can you get off me?" I pleaded.

"I'll move when I'm ready. I don't know why you in a rush anyway. Babe, you ain't going nowhere."

"Why dammit! I don't want to be here anymore. Neither the fuck do you, with ya cheating ass!"

"For the last fuckin' time, I ain't going nowhere, and neither are you." Then he whispered in my ear. "You mine, Golden... foreva!"

This nigga was crazy. It was like a switch had flipped, and his mind was gone like the wind.

"Bronte, what the fuck is wrong with you? You're really scaring me now with all this crazy talk." He pulled my face closer, making sure I gave him direct eye contact.

"You scared of me, Gold? Huh? You fuckin' scared of me now? Good! You know what makes me scared? The thought of losing you. I can't let you leave me, Golden. That's not an option. You feel me?" My heart was beating damn near out my chest. I'd never seen him act or talk like this before, and it was probably because he knew I was serious this time, even though he could sense my fear. He smiled at me and took his hand to rub it lovingly down the side of my face. I jumped when I saw it coming. "Babe, I'm not gon' hurt you." He smiled so sweetly. "You so beautiful." He felt me trembling. "Why you shaking like dat? You that scared... what, you cold or something?"

"Yeah, that's it... j-just a little cold... I mean, you have me pinned down on this cold floor, and I'm barely dressed."

"Yo' ass shouldn't be tryna get away from a nigga. Look, it's late. I'm tired. I know you tired. Let's go to bed."

Bronte slowly got off me and stood up. Then he put his hand out to help me get up. I saw that as my window of opportunity and took my legs and clipped him. His six-foot self fell flat on his ass. I got up and ran in the direction of the front door. The kitchen door would've been faster to get out, but I wasn't thinking and just ran the opposite direction of Bronte.

My hands were shaking as I hurriedly tried to unlock the door. I barely had on clothes and no shoes, but I didn't care. I just needed to go while I had the courage to. I finally got the door open. I only got to take two steps before Bronte was tackling me in the grass. I was about to scream, but he covered my mouth, reducing my sound to a groan.

"Hm... hm... hm..."

"Thought you could get away from me, didn't you? Yeah, now you listen to me. We gon' go back in this muhfuckin house without me having to get in that ass. You know why, because you gon' cooperate... understand?" I still was being disobedient because we were outside, and this was my chance to possibly draw attention to us for someone to come see. It was so early in the morning, no one was around, and all the lights in everyone's home were out. The more I tried to wiggle my way out of his grasp, he held onto me even tighter. "Oh, so you think this shit's a joke. You think I'm fuckin' playing witchu? Girl, I swear you keep this shit up, I'mma have ya ass under the ground. Stop fuckin' moving!" I stopped immediately. "You finally ready to cooperate?"

I hummed okay. I wanted to run so bad, but I was too afraid of him later shooting my ass. He held my hand with a tight grip, walking me along with him back in the house and up to the bedroom. My plan was to get under the covers and lay there until he fell asleep and then escape. He had my adrenaline pumping, and I thought for sure I was going to utilize this energy tonight. That was until he said something that clearly made me give things more thought.

"Lemme leave you with something before you fall asleep. When I tell you I love you, believe it. My love is mad crazy when it comes to you, girl. It's so fuckin' crazy, I'd kill a nigga for you... might even kill *you* and that nigga, and that ain't no bullshit," he said, smiling afterwards. "Now, where my good-night kiss at?" He had his lips puckered waiting. I didn't want to kiss him at all. Instead, I wanted to bite his fuckin' lips off, but I feared what might've happened if I tried it. I kissed his lips and turned opposite of him and laid down.

I didn't know what I was going to do. He turned and put his arms around me and cuddled up close. I laid there and silently cried, letting the tears fall as I contemplated shit. Why did things have to come to this? I didn't know who this man was anymore and didn't know how I was going to leave him exactly.

The crazy part of it all, was deep down inside, I wasn't sure if I really wanted to. He loved me, and I honestly loved him too. I did, with all my heart, but not this version of him. I wanted the Taye that made me feel special, appreciated, and so much more, but he left a long time ago to be honest.

Thoughts of the direction of my life flooded my mind. Another year older, but not another year wiser. I didn't know why I went along with getting dressed up to go out in the first place. Had I said no, we never would've been fighting because I wouldn't have been expecting him to come through with what he said.

It was silly of me to think since he knew how I felt about my birthday and never asked to take me out before, he wouldn't bullshit me on this. But it fell in line with everything else in my life, and all of it, I was tired of. I needed to get away, and right after he left in the morning, I would be leaving too. It was time I took a stand for myself in hopes of him noticing.

2

SEPTEMBER 05, 2005

It was early in the morning, and I awakened in the bed alone. I knew where Bronte was, but he wasn't far enough, and I couldn't let that discourage me from doing what I needed to do. I would've been more of a fool if I stayed and let that happen. Even though I still loved this man beyond his flaws, the truth was, the love I was getting wasn't enough anymore. I wanted more of what I knew he was capable of, but I was tired of trying to get something from him, he wasn't willing to give... at least to me.

I gave him everything I had emotionally, physically, and mentally. Yes, he provided for me since he didn't want me to work. He also gave me whatever I wanted, but that was just things to pacify me. Him putting a Band-Aid over a much larger wound. I couldn't do this no more. It was time to go, even if I had to force myself to get out of here. My hope was if that fear he felt of losing me became his reality, he would change for me. I had to take the risk and see.

I jumped out the bed and picked up my phone and called the cops first. I explained about our turbulent past and what I was trying to do, so they said they would send someone out. Then, I ran to the closet and started gathering some of my things. I got a few pairs of shoes, jewelry, and a few hand-bags. I left the car he provided and a lot of other things that were from him that he would try to take back.

I was pressed for time since I figured Bronte had gone to the corner store, his usual morning routine. That was my opportunity to make a run for it. I really believed if he got back and caught me trying to leave, he would lose it. God, I hoped the police would be here by then, because I just wanted him to let me leave, that's all... no arrest... just let me go peacefully.

I paused and wiped my tears that were steady flowing from all that was going through my mind. I was hurt by how his love had changed and now made me feel like I was a possession and not his equal. Although, if I'm being honest, I didn't think I ever was treated as such, but it certainly wasn't like this.

I questioned why it was so hard for him to love me the way he used to or let me go. I couldn't understand that, but I knew as much as this was hurting me to do right now, I had to go. I had to say goodbye for the sake of us. I grabbed his shirt and hugged it close to me, breathing in deeply as I closed my eyes and thought about what once was and what was about to be.

"Goodbye, Bronte."

I hung his shirt back up.

"Goodbye?"

"Shit!" I grabbed my heart. "You fuckin' scared me!"

"What you doing, baby?" he asked as he curiously eyed me standing there. "You tryna leave out on me? Tryna sneak and shit?"

I walked away from him and put the things I still had in my hand in my suitcase. Bronte angrily pushed the whole thing on the floor. Then he looked at me with his lips tight and eyes damn near popping out.

"Put dat shit back in the closet and get yo' ass downstairs so we can eat."

"No!"

His eyes grew wider as he tilted his head, like hearing my answer was disrespectful to him.

"Fuck you say?"

"I'm leaving," I stressed.

"Golden, how many times we gon' go through this? The only place you going is down those fuckin' steps." Seconds later, there was a bang on the door. It startled Bronte. "Who da fuck is that?"

"I'm sorry, Bronte. I had to do it."

Bang! Bang! Bang! "It's the police! Open up!"

His eyes bounced around my face as he tried to fathom

what I did. I betrayed him. That was the lowest form of disrespect.

"You called the fuckin' cops on me?"

"I didn't call them on you. I just wanted assurance that you would let me go."

Bronte answered the door. He looked like he hated me. I quickly came partially down the stairs. I saw one of the officers grab him and put his arms behind his back and asked him for me immediately.

"I'm right here! I'm fine!" I yelled in a panic. When that officer turned around and I saw who it was, I nearly shit myself. His eyes glared at me in disbelief too. Completely caught me by surprise. "I uh... I just want to be able to get my things and leave, so don't hurt him."

Having to watch how they emasculated Bronte, hurt me to my core, but seeing it also being done by someone I knew fucked me up even more. I never expected this. All I saw was hurt on Bronte's face and disappointment on Cortez's face. He stayed quiet and didn't let on that he knew me, which helped the situation. Bronte was quiet as well and didn't even put up a fight with him and the other officer as they held him, but I knew there was fury from within, the way I saw the muscles in his jaws twitch. He just looked at me with so much anger in his eyes while I peered back at him. Little did he know, I was in knots on the inside as well, for two reasons.

"Ma'am, can you go get your things please," said the other officer.

That broke our stares which made me go get my things. Once I came down, I noticed they no longer were holding him. He stood right by the door with tears in his eyes as I walked toward it. I never saw Bronte cry before, except for when he got caught cheating and I tried to leave him then. It freaked me out so much to see this time. I didn't know what to say, so I didn't say anything and walked out ahead of the police.

As soon as I was inside their car, my phone started buzzing. It was Bronte. The tears from my eyes emerged and ran down my face steady like rain. I decided to forward the call. I couldn't bear to talk to him at that moment, not to mention the gaze I kept getting from Cortez through his mirror. Too much was swirling through my mind, and seeing him was like another slap in the face. He just added insult to injury. I didn't need his pity stares.

That certainly didn't help, but I couldn't think about him. I barely could fathom the thought of leaving. As I looked straight ahead, I still wondered if I was making a big mistake. Bronte had been my life these past seven years. I never pictured it without him. I never wanted to, but it was only so much a person could take, and as bad as I wanted things to be different between us, I wasn't sure if they would ever be.

I knew I needed to leave and never look back, so why did I look. As we drove off, I saw Bronte out on the step, eyes fixed in the direction of the police vehicle as I was being driven away in it. I had to muster up enough strength to keep my mouth shut and not tell Cortez and his partner to let me out, because in that moment, my heart was telling me to go back. This really hurt, but I knew I had to be tougher than the pain and love sometimes hurt.

I had them drop me off over my girlfriend Kosha's house. She had been expecting me. When we pulled up, I had texted her to let her know that I was on my way in. She told me the door would be open. Of course, Cortez walked me partway up her walkway, carrying my things.

"I want you to take my card." He handed it to me. "Call me."

He had me more angered. My heart was broken enough, and I damn sure didn't need him trying to step in. I snapped in his face.

"Not now, Cortez. Fuck!"

"You got me all wrong." He tried to explain. "I'm only saying that in case you need someone to talk to."

"And you think it would make things any easier for me, by talking to *you*... so you could gloat in my face!"

"Golden, you know I would never do that to you. I'm just concerned. Use it or don't! But just know... I'm here." His eyes really focused in on me. "You hear me?"

He set my bags down and went and got back in the police vehicle. They pulled off. The minute I walked inside, my phone alerted me to a text. It was Bronte again. It read: *I know I fucked up on ya birthday and a whole lotta other shit before it, but that didn't mean I ain't love you Gold. That shit ain't gon' change, but now, the way I show love for ya fuckin' ass will. Know that shit!*

"What's wrong?" Kosha asked as I was done reading but still staring at my phone.

"Oh! N-Nothing." I evaded, trying to downplay my real emotions.

Part of that text scared me. It bothered me that he said the way he'd show love for me would be different. I think I'd gone too far this time, but this situation we were in wasn't my fault. He had to have known my leaving him was very hard for me. I was in such pain on the inside that all I wanted to do was crawl in the bed in a tiny ball and cry, but I had to save face in front of Kosha. She hated Bronte and was likely happy I left his ass.

"I know you're lying, but it's cool. Anyway, you can put your things in the spare bedroom. You know where it's at."

I started walking toward her stairs and stopped when my foot touched the first step. I looked at Kosha who went back to comfortably sitting on the couch.

"Thanks, Kosh."

"Girl, you know I'm glad you're here. I'll be here as well when you're ready to talk about that text."

I smiled at a minimum then continued on my way up the steps. All I kept hearing was his voice in my head and the different things he'd say to me but would show me something different. I knew I wasn't crazy for leaving. I was crazy for staying so long, but why did I feel so bad for leaving?

We'd had a tumultuous relationship, but even with all our ups and downs, I was always compelled to stay, or more like dickmotized into it, which was what I was going to miss the most.

I think that's why I got so crazy with thinking he was fucking everybody. The sex was *like that*, and to know that he gave what was mine away, made a bitch act cuckoo every now and then. It didn't help either that he owned the streets, so he always made sure his shit circulating properly, was a priority. I hated what he did. I always feared him getting arrested or killed, but I stayed out of it.

He made sure I didn't know shit anyway. Which was why I never knew if he had gone to handle business or was *handling bitch business*. I remember one-night, Bronte and I were up in my bedroom in the place I stayed before moving with him, having a heated discussion about some chick I saw him talking to at the club we had just left. He had claimed then, it was just business, but what I saw was something completely different.

"Oh! I'm seeing things. I'm seeing things? What the fuck was she doing touching your face, Taye?"

He was comfortably laying across the bed on his stomach, head lying flat on his cheek, and arms dangling over the edge with his eyes shut and not a care in the world about what I was saying.

"She didn't touch my face. You just seeing things like I said."

I crossed my arms and angrily drooped my eyelids at his

audacity. I knew what I saw, and he was not going to pull this Eddie Murphy shit again.

"You are one lying motherfucka! She had both hands on the sides of your face, smiling like a clown because she thought she was going to kiss you. That sure as hell ain't her business with you. I can't even go to the bathroom without ya ass flirting and shit with a bitch!"

"I know yo' ass ain't complaining. I can't even take you the fuck nowhere without you tryna fight and shit. You damn near scalped ole girl the minute you got over there. Yanked all her shit out, and for what? Nothing!"

"You think anytime I check a bitch it's for nothing. You keep it up, it's really gonna be over."

"Let it be over then!" he challenged.

"You would say that. You don't really care about me anyway, or else you wouldn't have cheated. I should've let it stay over then, with ya sorry ass!"

He breathed out all hard while looking in any direction but mine.

"Now we back on that again. You know I fuckin' care. I'm here aren't I?"

"Yeah! Being an ass! I honestly wouldn't care if you weren't." I yelled spitefully.

He didn't like that and got up from the bed and yoked me up like a child he was about to scold.

"So why the fuck I'm here now then? Huh? And I'm not gon' be many more of ya muhfuckas and sorry asses!"

I suddenly began to cry from anger while I tried to pry his hands away.

"Get the fuck off me!"

Kosha was over too at the time, since we had double dated that night. She was coming from the bathroom and saw us since the room door was open.

"Hey! What's going on?" Bronte quickly let go of me before she saw me hemmed up. She stared at me, concerned. "Golden, are you okay?"

"I'm fine," I said, fixing myself. "He was just leaving."

His head shot in my direction surprised.

"I was?" I looked away from him and said nothing. "I guess I'm leaving then."

"Golden, are you going to be alright?" Kosha asked again.

"She gon' be fine!" shouted Bronte, irritated. "Can you excuse us doe? I'm not done talking to her yet."

Kosha hesitated.

"I'll be in the sitting room with my friend and cell phone close. You may not call the cops to lock his ass up, but I sure will." She eyed him. "Would love the honor," she jeered.

She took her time walking out, body moving before her oval shaped gray eyes left his sight. Bronte slammed the door behind her.

"Fuck outta here!" he ranted on. He put his arms around me with his hands cupping my ass. "So, you really don't want me to stay here tonight?"

I wiped my tears away as I responded, still looking away from him.

"I want you to act right, but what I want and what I get never seems to match up."

"Alright, so that girl did have her hands on my face. She did it so fast I didn't have no time to react before you saw her. It was innocent doe. We were talking business. I wasn't going to let her do nothing to me. Plus, she saw who my boo was. You made sure of that," he stated. Then he smiled while squeezing on my butt cheeks, playfully, trying to get me to laugh. I wasn't amused in the least. I finally stared at him.

"You should've checked her!"

"You right! I shouldn't have let her be close to me period, but I honestly didn't know she was going to try anything."

His face closed in on me as he tried to bait me into a kiss.

"I'm tired, Bronte. I need to lay down. Alone!"

His head moved back quick as he processed my response before he let me go.

"Alright! I'll call you tomorrow."

"Don't bother."

"What? You said don't bother," he repeated while smiling. "You talking out ya ass right now, girl." Then he smacked it. "I don't know why you tryna play hard and shit anyway, but it's cool. I know you love me."

I remembered having a half a smile on my face since he showed how annoyed I made him when he went in to kiss my lips, but I shut it down. After that, he left. That was

Bronte's first time putting his hands on me. Little did I know, it wouldn't be the last time we'd get into it.

"Gold! You okay up there?" yelled Kosha, bringing me out of my thoughts.

"I'm good! Putting my things away!"

"I'm ordering take-out. You want anything?"

"No, but thanks!"

I had no appetite. It still wasn't real to me that I had left. When he cheated on me before, I wasn't living with him yet, but after some time apart, I forgave him and moved in afterwards. I sat on the bed and contemplated on what I had done. Mostly because my head and my heart weren't on the same page. Seeing that text made me wonder if I'd really lost him.

I knew Bronte didn't treat me the best, but I didn't treat him the best either. We both were hotheaded and didn't give a fuck when we got upset. But at least I was trying. Bronte wasn't, and his ways, I had enough, which is why I figured I'd stay with Kosha for a bit until I got my life back on track with hopes of him coming to his senses once I'd gone. Now, I wasn't so sure if what I'd done was the right move.

3

SEPTEMBER 30, 2005

"Golden, this nigga sitting outside in his car. He's really waiting for you to leave."

I walked over and peeked out the bedroom window where Kosha was. I had been miserable without Bronte. I was blowing up his phone and sending him text messages since we'd been apart. I wanted to communicate with him, know that he was okay and that we were still cool. I missed him. I didn't realize how much until he finally called me back and we talked.

Hearing his voice again changed my whole world, but something was definitely different. It made me think about what he said to me about not loving me the same. *Was he for real?* I wondered. I called him so much begging to see him that he finally came by. Of course, it would be when I was about to go out. When I looked out that window and saw my boo, my pussy tingled immediately. Damn, did he have an effect on me. The downside was I had to act like I didn't know why he was here in front of Kosha.

"He has a lot of nerve." I huffed.

"What are you going to do?"

"Nothing! We're still going out. I don't care if he's outside. His ass can stay out there all night for all I care."

I hoped me trying to save face in front of her was working. I wasn't for certain, but I had hoped Bronte came by here. Even with everything we'd been through, I still loved his crazy ass. Yes, I cared more than I let on around her, because I wanted her to think I was finally done with him. When on the inside, I was praying like crazy that things would change after enough time went by and he'd had enough of me being gone.

"You know good and well you don't mean that shit. You gon' be lucky to make it out of here tonight at this rate. You always let him talk you out of us doing something."

"In my defense, that depended on what was going on. Plus, *that* was before."

"Bitch, now you know that shouldn't matter. If we had plans, you need to keep them, not bail on me because he's being a jackass."

"My ex is not a jackass... to *you*," I emphasized. "He's *my* jackass, and he just loved him some Golden."

"He's *your* jackass, alright," she agreed. "An obsessed one.

I keep telling you to leave his crazy ass alone, but you just won't listen," she said as she walked away from the window.

"I'm not even messing with him anymore, so how can you say that?"

"Then why have you still been on the phone with him and texting each other like you never left? Not messing my ass!"

I opened my mouth, about to explain, but then I left it hanging open, not saying what I started to. I didn't think she realized it had been him, but it wasn't only him. I had also been talking to Cortez from time to time. He stayed checking up on me. Something she had lost touch with. Someone actually caring.

Kosha didn't have a steady boyfriend. She was just having fun dating. It had been some time since she'd had a long-term relationship. Her ex was serving a life sentence in prison. After that she shut down and hadn't committed with anyone seriously, since. I felt like she forgot what that was like to love someone so much.

"Are you ready or what?" I asked, switching it up.

I got mad. I wasn't trying to hear her shit any longer. I'd been with that man for seven years, and feelings, no matter how shitty a situation can be, don't go away just because we were no longer together. Regardless how she felt about my relationship. It was mine. She complained all the time about how he always had me suspecting him of cheating and how he ain't shit and knew exactly what he was doing by keeping me under his lock and key.

Bronte was not all that bad, and I was tired of her talking about him like that. Yes, he had his issues, but what guy didn't? He was just the overprotective type when it came to who he loved, and truth be told, I was the one having a hard time letting go. But one thing I was sure of, was not letting his presence change my mind about going out tonight. I knew that would really piss Kosha off, and I had to prove her wrong.

"Am I ready? I'm not the one that has a crazy ass stalker waiting outside."

"Come on. Let's go."

We went downstairs and out of the house. As soon as I locked the door, Bronte got out of his car. Once I saw him coming toward me, I took a deep breath. I had to pull it together because, damn! He was in all black, even down to his Timberland boots. He knew I loved when he wore black, and then he had a fitted cap on that just added to his fly. The effect he had over my mind, body, and soul was like kryptonite. I would succumb to his presence. I really needed now to be different.

"I'll be waiting for you in the car," said Kosha. She walked by Bronte and rolled her eyes at him.

"Hello to you too, Kosha," he teased with a chuckle as he shook his head while she walked by.

She gave him the finger. No love was lost there. I started rubbing up and down my right arm, a nervous habit.

"Bronte, I can't believe you're here."

"You been blowing up my fuckin' phone begging me to come talk. Now you fuckin' surprised."

"I just didn't think you'd show up, especially tonight since I told you I wouldn't be here."

He looked away from me and smiled. Something was brewing in his brain. He laughed to himself as he eyed me up and down.

"Why you wearing that shit?"

"It was a gift from Kosha," I replied while putting my hand on my hip, disliking his nerve since any other time, he'd love what I had on.

"You got other dresses you could've put on instead of having ya ass hanging out. Dressed like her hoe ass."

"This is no different from what I'd wear when I was with you. You never complained before."

"You know what? Wear whatever you want. It don't even matter no more. What you want, man? I gotta go," he said, looking at his watch.

"Really, Bronte? It's like that now?"

"You fuckin' made it like this!" he yelled.

"So it's my fault that you've changed and can't keep your damn dick in ya pants and treat me the way you used to treat me?"

"I guess that's why the fuck you left and called the cops

on my ass." He slightly leaned in my face. "You got what you wanted, right?"

I was trying my best not to cry, but anytime my emotions got the best of me, it was inevitable. I took a deep breath and remembered that Kosha was watching.

"You being like this is not what I wanted. No! I just want you to be honest with me and not play no games."

"Whoa, woah! First off, who's playing games. You wanted me to come here," he said boastfully. "I see why though. Got yaself all dolled up and shit. You wanted me to see you like this, right? So who's playing games, Gold?"

"Fuck you!"

I tried to quickly walk away from him, but he pulled my arm, yanking my body back.

"What I tell you about just walking away from me like that when I'm not done?" I stared at him holding my arm. That right there let me know he did still love me. He let me go. "I'm sorry. Go 'head and enjoy yourself, and even though I complained about what you wearing... you look real beautiful tonight."

My simple ass got all giddy and smiled so wide, cheesing. "Thanks!"

I watched him as he walked back to his car. Even though he didn't say it, I knew he still cared about me as much as I cared about him. I had made some headway. I got in that car so fast and happy as a schoolgirl getting noticed by her crush. Of course, Kosha had something to say.

"Took you long enough! I thought for sure he was going to talk you out of going, no matter how you claim he ain't ya man no more. 'Cause where I'm sitting, somebody was not having it."

"Girl, shut up!" I turned up the music in the car. "Ayeeee!" I sang. "We gonna get in here and turn *thee* fuck up! You hear me?" I was feeling good suddenly.

"Right," agreed Kosha. "Nothing but a good time tonight." We looked at each other and pointed. "No bullshit," we said at the same time and laughed. It was something crazy we started doing to confirm we were going to avoid bullshit from bitches. So, we called it before we went places and did things since trouble had a way of finding us at times, and we both were fighters.

My tolerance with bitches was non-existent compared to Kosha's, meaning my fuse was shorter than hers and didn't take much testing before it got blown. Nonetheless, we were two peas in a pod to an extent, which I think is why we got along so well. We looked damn good too, which would bring us a lot of attention, the times we would go out. That brought a lot of jealous bitches our way which in turn brought on fights.

According to Kosha, she got picked on a lot, growing up, for being light skinned with gray eyes and I got picked on for not having shit. When you get tired of fighting yo' momma for taking a "L", you learn real fast how to fight. We never set out to find trouble, but if it occurred, best believe we weren't backing down.

Kosha and I's body shapes were pretty close, too. Small waist, big ass, and thighs with grapefruit sized breasts. Some would misjudge that for us being too cute to know how to throw down. Once they ass got beat, they knew. No bullshit.

Bodies were wall to wall when we walked inside the *Glasshopper*. It was dimly lit, except for the multicolored lights that scanned the room from time to time. Once we hit the floor, I showed my ass, almost literally. It had been a while since I went out, which was with Bronte last, before my birthday debacle, but tonight, I was with my home girl, and we were doing the damn thing.

I ripped that dance floor up. Danced so hard, I needed a drink, so I went over to the bar. I was ready to buck when I saw Bronte sitting there conversing with a bitch. Felt like a bull seeing red, but like a street sign, stop wasn't written on me. The shock from him being here alone got me, but then seeing his chocolate happy ass sitting there talking to another female like he didn't just leave my side, made my temperature rise and my body hot, and not in a good way!

I strutted right over there, ignoring the men that were grabbing at my hand wanting to talk or get me back on the floor. I had another motherfucka to attend to and a bitch to dismiss. She was in the middle of talking when I stood right beside him and took his drink out his hand and drank some of it.

"Woo! That's strong... ugh!" I gasped. "My chest is burning. Bronte, that's not what I told you to get for me." I could tell the chick that was sitting there didn't care at all to see me or like what I said. The way her eyes scanned the both of us and her sudden laughter to herself, I was sure she sensed we knew each other well, especially since I said his name, which prompted her to stand up.

"Thanks for the drink, Bronte," she said.

She picked up her glass and with hesitance, walked off. I politely smiled and waved her on letting her know she was dismissed. I honestly came to the club with no intentions of causing trouble, but seeing a broad in my man's face wasn't the move and gave me reason to misbehave.

"Bye, bitch!"

She swung her ashy weave around and cut her eyes at me.

"Bitch!" she repeated back, angered.

"Yo, chill!" yelled Bronte at me. "Fuck's wrong witchu?"

By the time he turned to address the girl, she had started again on her way, which was what she better had done. She ain't want it. I stared at Bronte with a stale face.

"She's cute."

"Fuckin' gorgeous!"

"Excuse me?"

"Why you playing 'round with my drink and shit?"

"I had to fuck with it. It looked a little flat. You need something with more kick."

"That still didn't stop you from being thirsty, did it."

"I'll keep that in mind the next time you're blowing up my phone wanting your whistle wet."

"As you can see, I got plenty of other options."

"And so do I."

He didn't like that.

"You must wanna get choked tonight, right?"

"I do, and I am, but not from no one's hands," I toyed slyly.

"Yeah, okay. Keep talking shit to me."

He took a swig of his drink.

"Are you jealous?"

"I'm cool. What I gotta be jealous for? I'm chilling. You the one that came here disturbing me and what I had going on."

"No, I think you got that twisted because you knew I was coming here tonight. So, who's disturbing who?"

"I know yo' ass disturbing my shit, standing all close in that tight fitted mini dress. Cleavage all exposed, asking a nigga to run up in between it."

"That amongst other things," I admitted casually, while digging my fingers under my nails.

"Get away from me, man, before I drag yo' ass up outta here. I told you to go 'head and enjoy yaself, so why you over here in my fuckin' face?"

"Ooo the temperature done changed since we've been in here." I thought I'd take things a step further. I whispered in his ear. "I'm not wearing any panties either, in case you hadn't noticed."

Then I walked away with more of a switch than I already had, feeling my booty jiggling against the fabric of my dress. Never did get my own drink. I knew my thirst would get quenched. I went back out on the dance floor and back to shaking my fat ass. It didn't take him long at all to move the guy that was behind me and take his place.

I knew it was only a matter of time before he dropped his act and came to his senses. I knew Bronte too well, I just had to hang in there long enough until he got out of his pride being hurt. Plus, since we'd been apart, I was mad horny, and seeing him was another story. As I said before, Kryptonite!

Bronte was grinding on my ass as I was backing it up on him. Then he placed one of his big hands over my belly, keeping me pinned to him as we swayed to the beat as one. His handsome face was buried in my neck while he sucked on it in between dragging his tongue on my skin, then kissing me. My body was hot like fire and in need of being extinguished.

His free hand traveled under my dress, lending his fingers to slide right between my dribbling lips. My head leaned back as his subtle strokes had my pussy pulsating tremendously, while stimulating more of my essence. His lips were right there to offer me kisses, but I could barely kiss him back from panting at the destruction his fingers caused.

I was ready to be fucked in the worst way, and Bronte could tell.

"Let's get out of here."

He brought me out of my bliss and pulled me along. I knew I couldn't just leave because of Kosha. I tried to see if I spotted her as we headed to the exit, but it was so many people, that became impossible. I figured I'd send her a text. There was no way I wasn't going with Bronte the way my body was feeling. The minute we got into his car, I texted her letting her know I left and I'd see her later.

The second we got inside the house, Bronte pulled me into him and handled my lips. As we kissed, he quickly unfastened his pants, pulled them down, and hiked up my dress. I jumped up on his tall stature like a pole dancer, him holding me by my butt cheeks as we kissed. Suddenly, I felt his fingers plunge inside of the back entrance of my bum. "Uhhh." I moaned from the sudden sensation. With his legs restricted from his pants being down, he carefully walked us over to the couch while his fingers danced in my ass. I gyrated on them as they played that familiar nasty tune on repeat.

Next, I was laid out on the furniture with Bronte making a grand entrance. One of my legs dangled in the air against the back of the couch while the other hung listlessly off it as he grinded on me. He pulled my breasts out the top of my dress, releasing them from my bra, and bathed my nipples with his tongue. My hands dug into his back, me practically smothering him by pushing my titties further in his face. He bathed and fucked me so good, I bit his shoulder to free my aggression because I was about to cum. That drove him nuts.

"Bronte... I'm... Oh God! I'm cum... I'm cumming Bron... tayeee!" I strained to get out.

I heard him grunting too, and his nut shortly followed, leaving us both wiped out. Bronte took his shirt and his jeans off the rest of the way, then pulled me out of my dress afterwards and laid close to me on the sofa. His luscious lips connected with my skin again, nibbling and pecking on my neck.

"Bronte, babe, I need a minute."

"I'm not doing nothing." He soothed me while he continued to brush his lips on my neck.

"Like hell! You know exactly what you're doing," I muttered as I moved my head further back in enjoyment. That minute that was needed, came to a quick end when my cell phone started ringing. Bronte raised his head up quick, fast, and in a hurry.

"Who's that calling at this time?"

"It's probably Kosha." He sat up and grabbed my phone to look at it. "Really, Bronte!"

He handed it to me when he realized it was locked and I had a new passcode on it.

"Unlock ya phone and show me."

"What?"

"You heard me." I took my phone from him, climbed over

his legs, and headed for the kitchen, ass naked. He jumped up right behind me, fussing in his boxers. "Golden!" I kept walking till I got to the small wine refrigerator he got for me when he was being nice. I remained calm.

"Yes, Bronte?"

"Who was calling you?"

I poured myself a glass of wine and put the bottle back and set my phone down on the counter while he was giving me the evil eye. I was pretty sure it was Kosha, but I'd be lying if I said I wasn't worried about it being Cortez.

"Babe, calm down. I'm telling you it's no one but Kosha."

"Why you can't show me?"

I took a sip of wine before I responded.

"Show me the last call in your phone and I'll show you mine," I said, widening my eyes at him, waiting.

Bronte nodded his head.

"Alright!" Then he came up behind me and palmed both hands on my thighs and spoke near my ear. "Don't show me. It don't matter anyway. You just gon' pay for dat shit."

I was just pulling the wine glass away from my mouth again when he said that last part.

"What?"

I set the glass down on the island and stared at him once more as he eased himself in front of me with his eyes peering in my direction like a lion focused on its prey. He lowered his body in front of me before he placed his hands on my hips and showered my belly with kisses. Then he threw my right leg over his shoulder and his soft, full lips kissed my wet ones below. Just like that, he took my breath away and had my body trembling.

Then his tongue took a dip in my overflowing pool, further leaving me breathless. My hands automatically gripped his shoulders since all feeling in my legs was about to be non-existent. The way he handled my bud and sucked my juices like a vacuum had me trying to crawl away from him. That just made him freeze me in place even more to take his tongue lashing. His tongue continued to lap me up like a dog slurping water. My well was undoubtedly sprung.

Then he stood up, moved my wine glass out of the way, tossed my body on the cold counter, pulled his dick out, and fucked me effortlessly on the edge of it. He ended up pulling my legs to his sides, really sealing the gap. I couldn't do nothing but lean back, hardly able to hold myself up from being weak from his feasting. His thrusts grew stronger and damn near whip lashed my neck from his force running into me. This went on for some time before Bronte climaxed again, letting his seed spill all on my belly.

"Damn, you got some good shit!" he praised. He leaned in and kissed my lips. "My pussy," he bragged before walking out of the kitchen. I just laid there thinking about his words and the entitlement that rang in them. I loved it. It was his pussy. I dragged myself up and hopped off the counter. I was cold. My nipples were all hard, and I noticed his chocolate ass didn't even wipe his cum off me. I went and got a paper towel to clean myself off before I checked to see where Bronte went.

I didn't see him in the living room, so I figured he walked up the stairs. I grabbed my things off the couch and then went up to get in the shower. Noise from the bathroom caught my attention when I heard the water running from his room. He was turning the water off to get out just as I made my appearance.

"No! Leave it on," I ordered. He obliged before he got out. "Bronte, wait!"

"What's wrong?" he asked as he wrapped himself in a towel.

"I just wanna ask you something."

"What?"

"Do you still love me?"

He looked me in the eyes and ran his fingers down a few strands of my wavy hair.

"You know me well enough to know my word is bond. Anyway, you already know I got love for you. I don't even know why you asking that dumb shit." Then he smiled and chuckled like it was a joke before he walked out the bathroom.

I had to take a moment and let that sit. He had love for me. Like what the fuck was that supposed to mean? It was hard to know if he was serious since he still did not answer the question as far as I was concerned. Since I had the water running, I got in the shower and stopped myself from over-thinking. I knew he still loved me. Bronte couldn't live without me, which was why I was here at this moment.

When I walked back in the room, I saw Bronte texting on his phone. He set it down the minute I saw him.

"Who's that this late?" I asked, turning the tables on him.

"It's about business. Just bring yo' fine ass over here."

I raised my eyebrows, skeptical about his response. Hey, I was here and they weren't, so I dropped my towel I had on and got in the bed beside him. Before long, Bronte was knocked out. I could not sleep for wondering who he had been texting. Then I heard his phone chime again to another message.

I looked over closely in Bronte's face to make sure he was in a deep sleep before I eased out the bed and tip toed over to look at his phone. The message was on the front of his screen. Wouldn't you know. It was a bitch. That damn Jackie. The text read: *I wish you would stop ignoring my calls. I need to talk to you.*

I looked over at the son of a bitch. I didn't know what to think. Only because the text was something positive as far as I was concerned.

I whispered, "Obviously, if he's ignoring you, he doesn't want to talk to you, but why."

I wondered if it had to do with us. If I could've called her or responded, I would've did it for him. Suddenly, Bronte squirmed. I quietly set his phone down and slid back in the bed with him.

BRONTE BROUGHT me back to Kosha's in the morning.

"You know I could've stayed with you. You didn't have to bring me home yet."

"Nah, I got things to do today at the house."

"And I can't be there?"

"Look, Gold, I'm not gon' sit here and argue with you. You wanted to be here; well, here you are."

"Why are you treating me like this? I'm sorry, okay. How many times do I need to apologize? I just want you to stop fucking around on me, Taye, and treat me the way you used to when we first met. That's all!"

He looked at his watch. I hated when he did that shit to me.

"You holding me up, man."

I took my hand and mushed the side of his face, hard.

"Fuck you, Bronte!"

He hemmed me up by the top of my dress, making it lift my boobs.

"Put ya fuckin' hands in face again and I'mma shoot dat ass!"

My eyes narrowed in disbelief. I was floored that he said that to me again. We both were silent as he had me close to his face in a tight grip.

"I honestly thought you loved me, but if you can easily shoot me then maybe I did do the right thing by leaving."

He forcefully pushed me even more into the door as he let me go.

"I ain't got time for this bullshit," he said as he put his hands back on the steering wheel and looked toward the windshield.

"I ain't got time for your temper."

"But I have to deal with yours?" he refuted as he stared back at me.

"Yours is worse! I never told you to your face that I'd kill you."

"Why you keep going back to that shit?"

"Because you don't say that to people that you love. Plus, you have yet to say that you don't mean that shit."

"I do love you, and if me saying that has you watching what the fuck you do, then so be it."

"What about you with Jackie!"

"I don't even fuck with dat broad no more. She called out the blue."

I crossed my arms and leaned against the door in the car.

"Does she know that?"

The corners of his eyes crinkled as he responded with an attitude.

"Why you asking 'bout Jackie all a sudden. You been snooping in my phone, haven't you?"

"What if I did! What she need to talk to you about? She pregnant? Is that why you ducking her?"

"Get the fuck out my car, man. I ain't got time for this shit. Go!"

"Gladly!"

I abruptly opened the door and got out.

"Don't call me unless you've come to ya fuckin' senses," he concluded.

"Fuck off!" I meant that shit and quickly walked to open the door. It was around ten in the morning when I came in. Kosha was in the kitchen making her some breakfast. Still upset, I walked in there to speak. "Hey. Good morning."

"I see the cat has returned home from getting that dick."

I laughed so hard.

"Bitch, shut up!"

"Did you work up an appetite? You hungry?"

"I ate already. Thank you."

"I should be mad at your ass for leaving me last night, but I figured it must was for some dick because I know your ass was in need of it." I just shook my head with a smile. "You looked mad when you came in here though. Who did something to piss you off?" she asked as she was stirring her eggs.

"I don't want to talk about it."

"Yeah, you're mad."

"What time did you end up leaving last night?"

"Once it was over. I called you, but you never answered nor called me back."

"I saw it. Well, I'm about to go get dressed."

I turned to head out the kitchen when Kosha called me.

"Gold!" I turned back around. "You deserve so much better than Bronte. I just want you to know that."

"Why are we talking about Bronte? I wasn't with him."

"I didn't say you were. I just know you, and I know you miss his trifling ass."

I didn't say anything and went to get out of the clothes I had on. I knew Kosha meant well when she told me I deserved better, but Bronte made me happy. Even though he pissed me off with his ways, he wasn't always this intense. We laughed all the time, especially that first year when Bronte and I first started dating.

We met inside the store at the gas station. Kosha was about to drop me back off at my place, but we stopped to get gas first. I went in to pay for it, and there he was. He had no problem approaching me with his fine, dark, chocolate ass, and since I liked what I saw too, I let him have my number.

It was a wrap after that. We hung out all the time. It didn't take me long to fall for him at all. Bronte had always been confident and charming, but what surprised me was how spontaneous and romantic he could be. I remember when we first made love. Bronte had a surprise for me.

The location was in the garden on the rooftop of my building. He had planned a picnic up there. My eyes strolled around at the scenery. I saw a blanket laid out with rose petals on it and a picnic basket that sat on the table with romantic lighting surrounding it. The night was warm and humid with its own uncertainty in the air.

"Bronte! This is so... so unexpected."

"You like it?"

"Baby, I love it!"

I leaned in, and like a magnet, our lips were forced to touch. He pulled my whole body closely into him and devoured the pair. We went at it, tasting each other and enjoying the feel and the warmth of our bodies as we touched. I loved his touch. It expressed how much I meant to him. It was delicate and yet carried so much weight. As his hands squeezed my ass and pressed me more closely, I knew he wanted me just as badly as I wanted him.

When he bit on my lip as he kissed me, I knew it was because my lips were appealing, and he couldn't get enough of how sweet they were. When he kissed my forehead, it was endearing. I knew he loved me just as much as I loved him. All of this, I got out of his body language, and tonight it was speaking loud and clear. We finally came up for air and gazed into each other's eyes.

"I want you, Gold... bad!"

In that moment, he took me by the hand and led me over to the blanket that was sitting in the cut and helped me down on it. Bronte wasn't ashamed of his body at all, and he took off his shirt. "It's hot." The next thing I knew, we were both laid out, naked. As I laid there looking in his eyes, I let all my inhibitions go and allowed the moment to take over.

His pace was slow and steady. He felt so good inside of me as we rhythmically continued to grind. He definitely warmed me up. He kissed my lips. They were always so soft. He licked my ears... ahh yes... I loved his tongue game. His wide hands as they were *under me palmed my ass... fuck! I clenched down on his pole even more.*

"Squeeze this dick witcha pussy... yeah, just like that," he ordered. "Ahhh yeah." He moaned as I listened and did what he commanded.

All I was thinking was 'Kegel muscles don't fail me now'. Shit! His dick was so engulfed in my pussy there was no escaping until I came. My legs started shivering from this unexplainable feeling. With his eyes focused, piercing right through me, all I could do was moan while I dug my nails in his back to express my emotions. He just grabbed my ass tighter and put it on me even more, and I wanted it... all of it!

"Ahh! Ahh! Got dammit, Taye...mmm..."

That just sparked me up even more, and I pulled him deeper inside of me in one shot, taking it to the head. That move right there must've led him to the X spot because he went crazy after that, trying to hit the target. I smiled to myself. I had him right where I wanted him.

"Aww fuck!"

He had his ugly face on. The one where I could tell his mind was blown. Now the tables were turned. Instead of him focusing on me cummin', he couldn't stop focusing on it happening for himself. He was mesmerized by my melting pot. As we fucked on a blanket outside with plants surrounding us and mother nature watching us, Bronte's volume continued to become a little louder. I could tell the feeling was too great. His facial expression looked like he wanted to cry.

I wanted to see some tears too, so I grinded on him harder, increasing the intensity. I sweetened his pot of Gold and put my legs on his shoulders so we both could cum this way. I was so wet Bronte slid out of me one good time from my legs now being up on him. I wanted him to hurry up and put it back in. I was a fiend, addicted after my first few hits.

Instead, he teased me with the tip and rubbed it up against my clit. He knew I was close to climaxing before his dick slid out and that I eagerly wanted him back inside of me. He read my eyes and unselfishly put it in. I knew what he was doing, buying himself some time since he didn't want to cum yet. He kissed me quickly, sucking my lips, tugging them before he went back to fucking me. Moans of enjoyment filled the air. A few slow strokes before the grand finale, and we both were erupting and left panting from the rush.

Drenched in our love, we laid there breathing erratically. I looked at the sky while Bronte was laying on me with his head down on my shoulder. I couldn't believe I was naked outside on the damn rooftop having sex. I liked the fact that he was on top of me, now that I cared about my body being exposed. Bronte's body covered me up. After a minute, I had told him to move because his tall ass was heavy. His sweaty body peeled away from mine, and he situated himself beside me.

"You okay?"

"No, I need something to cover me now." *I scooted over closer to Bronte so I could pull the blanket on my side over me more. We only had the one. Bronte moved some to give a little more of the* cover. "I guess you don't care about being seen naked like that, huh?"

"I don't give a fuck! I was naked not too long ago when I was blowing ya back out. I'm s'posed to be worried about it now?"

I looked at my arm.

"Did you just feel that?"

"What?"

"I think it's about to rain."

Bronte started kissing on my neck.

"I guess mother nature wanna get wet too."

"Leave it to your ass to say something like that. We better go inside."

"For what? Baby, we not done."

"Bronte, I just told you it's about to rain."

"What dat mean?"

"I'm not staying out here and getting my hair wet."

"Why not? It's already fucked up." Then he ran his hand through it, making it messier. "Whatchu gotta say now?"

"Your ass is fired. You're not getting no more of my goodies."

"Man, I'll take dat shit."

"I'd like to see you try. I'm going inside." I was about to get up, but Bronte pushed me back down. "Stop!"

"Nah. We not finished."

"Bronte, it's about to rain. I'm serious! I don't want to get my hair wet. Can't we go fuck inside? Damn!"

"No. I want ya sexy ass out here."

I gave him a fake smile since I didn't share his sentiments anymore.

"See! I'm feeling more rain drops. Please, baby?"

Bronte was staring down at my pussy as it peeked out of the cover.

"I bet dat shit would really be wet." Then he tried to sweet talk me. "Alright, I'll make a deal witchu. If you stay out here with me a lil' longer and put up with the rain, next time we together I'll cook for you."

"Hmm. I don't know, Bronte. Your cooking's not as good as my pussy."

"Aw dat's fucked up," he said with a laugh. "I bet ya ass stay out here and get fucked doe."

"Bronte, the only way you're getting inside of this is if you take it, because I'm leaving your naked ass right here and going inside."

I tried to get up once more but never succeeded. Nor did I really try. Bronte pinned my arms down, moved the covers and sat his naked ass on top of me. I was pretending like I wanted him to get off me by resisting him. The drops started to spit out more and more. Bronte started licking the rain as it fell on my breasts.

His touch weakened me and made me relax real quick. I watched him as he let his tongue work all over my nipples as it collected the drippings from the precipitation. He was making my pot of Gold storm explicitly. I began to quiver as the sensation gave me tingles, combined with the coldness of the misty rain I never saw coming.

My man kissed down to my navel and then continued to my vaginal lips. His kisses had me squirming all over the place. Then came that first lick that I was anticipating. I gasped for air as his tongue and his lips feasted on my love. He dipped his tongue deep inside my melting pot and bathed it in my pool of nectar. The more he sucked, the more I dug into his shoulders, pushing him away, falsely wanting to evade the feeling.

Bronte suddenly stopped. He got up and stuck his dick inside of me. I cried out sounds of sexual gratification as he filled my insides. He gave me a few quick strokes and then pulled out. I laid there, dripping wet, looking in his eyes, still wanting him. As my body was in between his legs, he eased up to my face and played with his dick on it. He watched me smile as I watched his enjoyment. He went for my mouth, but I closed it, playing with him. He rubbed the tip across my lips, glossing them. He was turned on, and his look took on a seriousness.

"Take it." I gladly opened wide, and he put his dick in my mouth. I squeezed him in my jaws and gave a quick blow with the first stroke. Then he pulled it out and slowly fed it to me, sliding it back in again. I licked the head toying with the bullseye first, then sucked the crown of it. "Ahh." he groaned. "Yeah, baby, take my shit." He then pushed it in further in my throat. I sucked him, savoring him as my mouth gave the massage.

Then Bronte reached back with his right hand and fingered my pussy. I was starting to lose focus because he was about to make me cum again. I wasn't ready. My body was saying yes, but my mind wasn't. I didn't want this feeling to end yet. I had to react. I took his balls in my hand and methodically started massaging them. I could tell that was bringing Bronte close to his nut.

There was no escaping mine. As his pleasure heightened, my pleasure soared, and before you knew it, I was cummin' all over his hand. Mixed with the misty rain, Bronte took his fingers and put them in his mouth delighting in my flavor. He noticed me sleeping on the job at that moment. His dick woke my mouth up with one swift stroke. I wasn't ready for it and almost choked.

He laughed at me while he gave me a minute to clear my airway. I showed him who was going to have the last laugh. I formed my hand in a tube shape around my lips and told him to come inside. My hand ushered his dick right into my mouth. A few strokes like that, and Bronte was a goner. He was giving me a mouthwatering treat before he knew it. I gave him a mind-blowing experience he would never forget. Bronte got off his knees and laid back beside me. I took the edge of the blanket and wiped my mouth off. Then, I turned on my side to face him.

"You're paying for my hair appointment, right?"

He lifted his head, sweating profusely as he looked at me.

"Golden, doing shit like dat, I'll pay for whatever you want... damn, girl, you good."

"This was special. I can't believe I let you talk me into doing this. Do you think anyone can see us? Or even saw us? They could've come up those stairs and us not even know it."

"I don't know, but we probably should be getting outta here and going inside."

I cut my eyes at him.

"Oh, so now you wanna go inside."

"Yeah, wanna take my time washing you up."

We did just that and enjoyed the rest of the night together. He even cooked for me since the rain ruined the food in the basket. That motherfucka made me happy, but Bronte did change, and it wasn't for the better. I guess the faster I accepted that, the better. So why couldn't I?

4

OCTOBER 31, 2005

Today was Halloween. Kosha was dragging me out to a party, and of course, you had to wear a costume. I refused to spend money on one, because I really didn't care to go, but to my surprise, Kosha brought me one. I was going as Cat Woman—her smart-ass idea, and she was a Playboy Bunny. Wasn't feeling that shit at all, but I got ready and then we went on our way.

The party was located at the *Sanctum Hotel* in the city of *Iaburg* where Kosha and Bronte lived. We headed to ballroom one where the party was being held. It was so many people in there, and everybody looked good! I never saw so many unique costumes in my life. One girl had on this cute mummy one. Her white dress looked like bandages wrapped around her. Then she had her arms wrapped in bandages, her head, and some white knee-high boots that looked ribbed like bandages. Her whole get-up was fly.

"Come on, girl! Let's go dance," Kosha suggested, all excited.

"You go 'head. I'll join you in a bit. I'm going to have a seat over by the bar."

She frowned at me before bobbing her way to the dance floor. I wanted to leave. As nice as this place was, I didn't feel like this shit. This wasn't me, so I wasn't in the mood for it. Part of me was bummed out too, because I hadn't heard from Bronte since he told me to get out his car.

I broke down and called him, even sent him messages. I didn't get any text messages or any phone calls from him in return. That shit beat me down hard. He never even read my messages. He wanted to be like that, fine! My fear was that he was locked up, which could've been why I hadn't heard from him. At least that was what I told myself to ease the pain of him ignoring me.

"Care to dance?" I looked behind me and saw this big ole Caucasian penis standing there. I didn't know how I missed that spectacle coming in here, but I died with laughter. "What?" he asked innocently. "Don't even act like you haven't seen *me* before."

I was bent over still laughing. He caught me so off guard. I was done! Finally, I collected myself to answer this fool.

"Um... I can honestly say, I've never seen anything of your type before."

The length of his body was the penis with his head placed in the tip, uncovered only in the front to showcase his face. The ball sack was dangling near his feet.

"Well, I've seen plenty of cats, that's for sure, but you—" I began laughing again, which stopped him for a second. "Damn!"

"Okay, what uh..." I smiled, shaking my head, still taken by the sight of him. "What made you come over here and ask me to dance? I'm sitting, as you can see, but it's plenty of other people to choose from."

"I know, but I only chase cats, and you," he underlined, "are a rare breed. Besides, I think we'd make magic happen out on the floor."

My lips by now were pressed inward, trying to hold it together. I mean, I loved penises, but it was nothing attractive about this blow up one, which was why I laughed so much. He was funny though, and I needed a laugh.

"You know what, against my better judgement, I'm going to dance with you. Fuck it!"

"Ooo, don't say that to my dick. You're making it really hard."

"Let's go, dickhead," I said with a head shake and eye roll at his continued humor.

"For once, I'm not offended." I laughed. "I'm Big Ben, by the way," he said, offering his hand to shake as we walked. That made me laugh too.

"Golden. Nice to meet you."

"The pleasure is all mine." I cut my eyes at him again. "Seriously! All jokes aside. I think you're a very attractive cat... I mean woman."

"Thank you."

The minute we got on the dance floor, people started cheering and egging me on to ride him. These people were out their fuckin' minds. I was too, out here dancing with a big ass dick. Then Kosha came behind him, humping the back of him. Once she got started, I really showed my ass. I went ahead and let loose too.

I got low and played with his low-lying balls. Kosha was sliding down his shaft with her backside by now. His ass was working up a good sweat in that costume. His face was saturated. He couldn't handle us. I threw it back on him to fuck with him even more. He may have said he chased cats, but he wasn't used to this pussy cat being thrown at him. I could tell.

Then I was pulled away by a Batman looking costume, but it was all black. I later discovered he was dressed as the Dark Knight. This motherfucka had a physique on him. All I could see was his eyes, mouth, and chin. He had facial hair too. All rang familiar, but I wasn't completely sure who it was. The lighting in the room wasn't bright, so that also made it hard to really know.

All I knew was his ass could take me to his bat cave. He held me in his arms like he owned me. The way his arm cupped my back, bringing me into him, and the way his eyes had my attention, I couldn't move. The music was a fast song, and yet, he had my one hand in his, slow dancing.

"So, you pulled me in your arms to dance and not talk to me?" I asked as I tried to figure him out.

"My actions didn't speak loud enough for you?"

Damn! Who is this guy? His voice isn't familiar.

"Actions? What? That you... you wanted to dance with me," I replied sassily.

The corners of his eyes wrinkled as they took on a different tone.

"You're too beautiful to be dancing with that dick."

"Ohhh, and you figured you could do better?"

"No comparison."

"So that's a yes?" I surmised.

"Guaranteed," he said with a firm eye. That made my core swarm with butterflies. I didn't know who he thought he was, but dammit, I liked it.

"Thank you."

"For?" he asked without taking his eyes off me.

"Saying I was beautiful."

"You're welcome."

"Is this your thing? Pulling women away from their dance partners to dance with you?"

I got a hint of a laugh out of him.

"Definitely not my thing. My interest lies where I'm standing only."

I put my face closer to his, trying to get a gage of him from his eyes, but he moved his head back.

"Do I know you? Your eyes seem familiar."

He smiled, and it made my heart smile for once tonight.

"Believe me. You don't know me." Then I felt this vibrating. It was his phone that was clipped on his bat belt. He looked at it. "Excuse me. I'm sorry. I have to see about this."

"Sure!"

"Thanks for the dance if I don't make it back."

Please make it back. Then he dashed off. I felt let down suddenly. I didn't even know why. I was only in his presence a short period of time, but it was nice... seemed familiar. I was comfortable with him. Damn! He took my mind off Bronte. Then just like that, thinking about him taking my mind off Bronte, brought thoughts of him back.

I went to get a drink at the bar. I truly needed one after all that shit. I couldn't even say where Kosha's ass was. I was sure she was somewhere in here enjoying herself. I got my drink and sipped on it as I looked around the room to see if Batman would reappear. I didn't even get his name. That just pissed me off for even wanting it.

"Hey, bitch!" Kosha came over, looking tired out. "This is for you."

She gave me a napkin with a phone number on it.

"Who's this from? Don't tell me Ben gave it to you becau—"

"No, that handsome ass Batman gave it to me to give you."

I grabbed her wrist.

"What?"

My heart started pounding in my chest.

"Please call him, because if you don't, I will."

I started blushing.

"I thought he left."

"He was leaving, which was when I saw him, and he asked if I could give that to you."

I looked at the napkin again. How'd he know to give it to you?"

"We were dancing together before he swooped you away. It was obvious we knew each other."

"He didn't even leave his name. Did he at least ask you what mine was?"

"Nope! I assumed both y'all knew that shit. Oh well! Maybe he wants you to call him Batman," she joked.

We both started laughing, leaning on each other. That really put a smile on my face. It was a bit reminiscent of a time when I went out to eat and unexpectedly saw Cortez.

"Have you decided on your choice of drink?" The waiter was interrupted by a fellow colleague that whispered him a message. He returned his focus to me. "It seems the gentleman at the bar on the end has requested to pay for your expenses this evening."

I answered with a hint of surprise.

"Oh really?"

My first thought was what clown wanted to impress me now, but I decided to accept the offer. When I curiously looked to see who the gentleman was, I couldn't help but to blush when I real-ized it was the one and only Cortez.

He spotted me looking and raised his glass with a smile. Not the distraction I needed tonight, amongst others from him. None-theless, I figured I'd take it. I had just broken up with Bronte, hurt because he cheated, and I wasn't in a good head space. I had been trying to keep Cortez at arm's length, but then I thought maybe the disruption tonight would do me good. I looked to my waiter.

"Would you mind thanking him for me, and also telling him I'll make sure to make it worth it." I could tell my response made my waiter feel a bit uncomfortable. "On second thought..." I wrote my response down. "Can you hand this to him for me instead, please?"

"As you wish."

Cortez read it, and his face showed he was very pleased. My waiter came back to take my drink order. He recommended their Poinsetta made with Cointreau, Cavit Prosecco, and Cranberry juice. He said it paired well with the seafood, which was on my radar. He came back with it and a napkin with writing on it that read: **I already know it'll be well spent :)**

He was right about that. I was going to make the most of this moment. I was suddenly feeling frisky, so I started out with the fried oyster appetizer. It was accompanied by Cortez. As it was being placed in front of me, I was asked a question by him.

"Do you mind if I sit here to make sure that first bite is to ya liking?"

The waiter's eyes strolled over to mine, curiously looking, waiting to hear what I was going to say back.

"Can you give us a moment? I'll be ready to finish ordering soon."

"Sure! I'll be back over shortly."

I finally responded to Cortez.

"What are you going to do about it, if it's not?"

"Make sure you're nothing but satisfied. What else."

He was paying, so I figured I owed him at least that much.

"I guess you can have a seat," I teased, displaying a hand gesture. I eyed him suspiciously. "What are you up to, seriously?"

"Why I gotta be up to something?" He refuted with a huge smile afterwards.

"Because you're acting like you're up to something."

"I'm not up to nothing but being here with you tonight since we're both here."

"Stop playing!"

"Look, you know I like to make you smile and laugh. That's all this is." His tone changed. "But I'm glad you allowed me to hang out with you tonight. I just want us to enjoy a good meal and each other's company. Love, is that alright with you?"

"Love? I've graduated to love now?"

I had to mess with him.

"You've always been someone to love, but you be playing games."

"I think that's more your department. Coming up in here sending notes on napkins."

We both started laughing.

"Like I said before, I just like to make you smile..."

The waiter came back, interrupting us so I could put in for my dinner meal. Cortez ordered another drink and changed up the subject, telling me he had eaten already at the bar; he was just waiting for dessert.

"Dessert sounds good. That is, after I've finished the main course."

I took a bite of an oyster. Cortez watched me as I tasted it.

"How is it?"

I chewed with my mouth and eyes closed, savoring the flavor. Then I picked one up and popped it in his mouth.

"You tell me how it is." He chomped it down. "Well?"

"It's delicious."

"I'm even more excited now about the main course. Would you care for another?"

"That's all you. Maybe we can share dessert."

I looked at him like he was crazy.

"I don't know about sharing my dessert."

"Why not? I'd share with you without a problem."

"I didn't say it was a problem. It's just that if it's as good as this food, you'll have to make it worth my while to share."

"So what I gotta do to make it worth yo' while then?"

"It wouldn't be any fun if I told you, now would it? So... I guess you'll have to figure it out," I said before having another bite.

"Something I do best." He watched me take a sip of my drink to wet my palate a bit. "Oysters getting to you?"

"Mm, you could say that."

"Honestly, I think it's me getting to you."

"If you have to think, I guess the answer is no."

"And if you have to guess, that makes that shit a definite yes."

I laughed. He had me there. I didn't have a comeback, so I sipped on my drink again. The waiter came with my meal. Cortez had already gotten his drink. I had ordered the Macadamia Crusted Grouper with jumbo lump crabmeat, asparagus, and hollandaise sauce.

I nearly had an orgasm just looking at it plated. I dove into the crabmeat first. It was amazing! Then I offered Cortez some.

"Would you like me to plate a little of this for you?"

"I'm good. I'd rather sit here and watch you eat."

"I just feel so rude eating alone in front of you."

With his arms now resting on the table, he leaned forward and spoke alluringly low-key.

"It's been uh, many a times I ate alone in front of you and you watched," he toyed, showing his amazing smile. That was not the visual I needed right now. He leaned back, pleased, relaxing both hands on his stomach. "I told you I ate though. I'm just waiting till you get around to dessert."

"Is that really all you're waiting for?" I asked as I brushed my bare foot up and down his leg that was hidden under the draped dining table.

"Definitely! I need that cake... can't seem to get enough of it." He leaned inward once more and spoke with discretion. "Plus, it's been a while since I've had it... you feel me?" He grabbed my foot as it was on the rise and held it between his legs under the table.

I mouthed emphatically, "I feel you," before grinning. I had to remember not to smile so much. I didn't want to let him know how much I was enjoying this, so I stuffed some food in my mouth.

"I might not have any room for dessert after eating all this."

"Doggy bag it," he suggested while giving my foot a thorough massage.

"You don't enjoy it as much if you don't eat it right away."

"It depends on what you get. It has to be the right thing... to keep," he added, as he grinded his knuckle from my heel to my toes.

I loudly huffed from the unexpected pleasure, so I slyly started clearing my throat to camouflage the sound in case anyone heard me and started staring. I gathered my composure to clearly speak.

"So, what do you suggest that be?"

His hands returned to the table and he picked up the dessert menu and looked it over analyzing it.

"Lemme see here..." I smiled and rolled my eyes at his playfulness. "You could never go wrong with the chocolate truffle layer cake. Got white chocolate ganache in it. Shid, warm that thing up... mmm, girl, that's an explosion waiting to happen."

"I do like white chocolate explosions."

His eyes smiled back.

"They got Apple Crisp... now that shit's incredible too. Put some ice cream on it... caramel sauce... whipped cream..." he looked at me. "Nuts... you'd enjoy that like it was the first time it was put in front of you."

;t time, huh?"

,ded his head.

first."

"I'm intrigued."

"So, what you waiting on? Let's get it."

"Let's."

"I'll be right back."

Cortez returned with a container for my leftovers and a bag in his hand.

"What's that?"

"Dessert. Where you parked at? I'mma meet you at ya car."

I told him, then we left out separately. When we met up, Cortez told me he wanted to talk for a minute."

As soon as the doors shut, he set the dessert down on the center console in front of us and madly kissed me. It was so intense it made me fall back on the door, making me bump my head on the window. We stopped kissing and looked at each other laughing.

"You alright?"

"Yeah, I'm fine," I said, rubbing the spot.

"I'm sorry. I've been wanting to do that all night," he bragged. "Without you hitting ya head though."

I giggled.

"I know. Apology accepted."

"How 'bout we get out of here."

I figured, on second thought, maybe he was the distraction I needed.

"I guess I'll be following you tonight."

"Haven't steered you wrong yet."

He talked a lot of shit, but damn could he back it up. That was a fun night. Cortez was a completely different experience than Bronte. I was always waiting for shit to hit the fan, but it never did. He never raised his voice at me, put his hands on me, or even disrespected me in any way. He was everything I wasn't used to.

Then when he wanted to take things beyond what I thought was us having fun, I got scared and ran. Getting this napkin was just like something he would do, but the guy said I didn't know him. Maybe I didn't. Since I didn't have any pockets, I tucked the napkin in my breast. I just hoped I wouldn't sweat on it and smear the digits.

"Where was your ass coming from anyway?"

"I had just got finished talking to a hot mac daddy that also gave me his number, although I had it the minute he approached me."

I looked around the room.

"Is he still here?"

"If you see a pimp with a cheetah printed hat and fur around his jacket, that's him."

I laughed so hard.

"What's his name?"

"Girl, Jerome!"

"Hahaha!" This bitch had me in tears. "No, it's not, Kosh! Stop playing!"

"I'm playing. His name is Javar. His costume got him looking like Jerome's ass from Martin."

"I can imagine. Can we go now? I've had enough of this shit."

"Yeah, me too."

When we got to the house, the minute I got out of the shower, my phone rang. I started not to answer it because I didn't recognize the number, but I answered it.

"Hello!"

"Yo! What's up!"

This voice was a surprise.

"Bronte?"

"Oh, now you don't know me?"

"How I'm supposed to know this you? This ain't the number you usually call me on."

"So, who else you expecting to call?"

"Damn sure not you. I haven't heard from you since you dropped me off. Now you're calling me."

"Look, I lost my phone. Plus, I ain't even been here in town, but I been missing you like crazy. Now I'm back, I wanted to call you and apologize."

"You couldn't have called and apologized while you were gone?"

"Yeah, I could've, but it was best if I didn't. I was handling my business, and you know how I feel about things when it comes to that. But I'm sorry for the way I left things."

"I hear you, Bronte."

"I'm serious. What you been doing?"

"Kosha dragged me out to a Halloween party. I'm just getting back."

"Halloween party? You into those now?"

"No, but I wasn't into my birthday either, but that didn't stop you from wanting to do something that never happened, now did it?"

"Alright! You got dat. I don't even wanna get back into all that. Won't you come here though, so I can see you. I wanna talk to you."

"Sure you do."

"Nah, I'm serious!"

"It's late, Bronte, and I just got out the shower. I was 'bout to go to bed."

"Come sleep over here. Come on... I miss you, man. We don't even gotta do shit. I just wanna hold you and feel ya body against me." Him saying that gave me tingles. I wanted to be strong. I wanted to say no, just to teach him a lesson for ignoring me, but I couldn't. I needed to be next to him too and know what he wanted to talk about. I went silent on the line while I thought about being near him. I guess my silence took too long. "I'm on my way."

"Okay."

I got myself together and went to spend the night with my baby. I was glad Kosha was asleep so she wouldn't see me leaving with him. He stayed true to his word and held me all night. It was nonintrusive and beautiful. Early morning was a different story. I was sleeping on my stomach when I felt hands discreetly sliding my panties down. It woke me, putting a smile on my face. I knew his *"we don't even gotta do shit"* wasn't going to last. Although, I had an agenda of my own. He just beat me to the morning rush.

Next thing I felt was my behind being saturated and rubbed with oil. His hands felt so warm and soothing as I just laid there and enjoyed the massaging. Then I felt his tongue strategically traveling down the split in my ass. I poked it out even more as I gasped from the tingling sensation that inhabited my body. Just then, his face went underneath me, and he buried it in my pussy, sending me over the top.

He had my legs spread so wide as he manipulated my bud, continuously flinging his tongue upon it then tugging at it before slurping up the drizzle I had to give. My body trembled as I moaned while he handled what was his. I came in no time. Then Bronte got up, leaving me on my stomach, and fucked me from behind. Once he was well fed and had spooned with me for a bit, he dropped me back to the house again, not letting me stay with him.

"I'll see you later alright?"

"What you about to do, Taye?"

"Me and Spice got a shipment to see about. That's all you needa know." He leaned over and kissed me. "I'll call you when I'm done."

I got out and walked to the driver side and spoke to him through the window.

"I could've stayed at the house you know."

His expression dulled.

"Are we gon' go through this every time I drop you back off here?"

"I just want to know what we're doing?"

"I'm dropping you off. That's what we're doing."

"You know what I mean. When did I become just a fuck to you, Bronte?"

I could see the anger in his eyes about to cause his mouth to be foul.

"You ain't just a fuck, but what you are is starting to get on my fuckin' nerves."

"Why? Because I just want some answers?"

"I've answered ya fuckin' questions. What more you want me to say?"

"See! That right there. Your temper. You just can't help yourself."

"I wasn't even mad until you started on ya bullshit."

"I just miss you! I'm sorry for calling the cops to come. I'm sorry for leaving. I just want us back!"

"Do you trust me, Golden?"

My eyes bored into him at the mere fact that he even asked me that.

"Babe, I'm trying my hardest to trust you, but Bronte, you haven't made that easy for me."

"You find what you were looking for?"

I tore my face up even more as I tried to figure out what he meant.

"What are you talking about?"

"I'mma let you think about it."

Then he pulled off while I was still leaning on the car, damn near taking me with him.

"What the fuck, Bronte!" I yelled as he just left me there. I was fuckin' heated. His hot and cold attitude had gotten on my last nerve. The only thing I could think he was talking about was me looking at his damn phone. I could've sworn he was asleep, but what took me for a loop even more was the fact that he didn't even try to stop me from looking. He wanted me to see, but why?

I got my mind straight to go in this house. When I walked inside, I didn't see Kosha. I figured she must've been sleeping since I saw her car was here. I felt relieved as I walked up to the bedroom. She would've picked up immediately on the mood I was in and automatically thought I was out with Bronte. The minute I threw myself back on the bed, Kosha was in my doorway.

"Bitch, where ya ass sneak off to?" Her light gray eyes brightened with excitement. "Were you with Batman?" She looked so hopeful. After the bullshit I just went through with Bronte, I wished I had been with Batman.

"No."

Her stare was now a mix of disappointment and curiosity.

"No? Where ya go then?"

"Oh, after we had got in, I couldn't sleep, a Sheridan called wanting to go out for drinks, I went with her and just stayed over there."

"I don't know why you hang out with that sometimey cockroach."

"Shut up, Kosh!"

Sheridan was exactly that, which was why I could use her as a cover all the time. But honestly, I hadn't spoken to or seen Sheridan in years. I met her at the room share I used to stay at. Kosha was cool with Sheridan until she noticed how she only came around when she wanted something. I never had shit to give anyway before I met Bronte. I worked cleaning offices part-time since that was what I was good at, but what little I did have, I was always glad to assist. One thing I was not was selfish.

Hell, my life wasn't shit, so why not help someone else reach whatever they were aspiring to be. But her asking got worse once she saw I had plenty when I was with Bronte. I gave her rides to work, money for groceries at times, or a bill if necessary. Then once Bronte and I broke up for a period of time, Sheridan was nowhere to be found. But when we got back together, I really didn't see her anymore since I ended up moving in with Taye.

She never even called me, and I still had yet to hear anything about Sheridan or her whereabouts. But I never told Kosha that. I just let her think we continued to keep in touch, and from how her face was all contorted, she didn't like hearing I was with Sheridan. She walked in the room and stood in front of me with her arms folded and glared at me in silence for a few seconds.

"Fuck that bitch! I'mma need you to do one thing for me, and that is to call Batman."

"Kosh—"

"No, Gold! I don't want to hear it! Give that man at least one shot. For me," she stressed. "I know you liked him last night. Damn! You so hung up on that lizard ass muthafucka that treats you like shit when you could have a real man treating you like a queen. Well, I'm not going to let you walk away from this guy without at least seeing what he's about, because lawd knows the one you keep fucking with ain't shit."

"I'm going to give him a call today. Damn! I was doing it anyway, so you didn't have to tell me to. And stop talking about Bronte. I'm so over you criticizing him all the time. It doesn't and it won't change the way I feel about him, but I *am* tired of you coming for him."

"Then stop fucking with him! If not, long as we friends and I see how he treats you, you're going to always hear my fucking mouth! Bitch don't give a shit how you feel. Just like he doesn't!"

"I'm not even messing with Taye though," I defended with my face distorted and hands flared trying to convince her.

"And my ass ain't black. I bet the minute that black tarantula come crawling back I know you're going to be there, but I hope you won't, and riding the wings of Batman." She demonstrated with her arms flapping.

"I hate you!"

"Call Batman!" she demanded before leaving the room.

I needed a shower. My body was worn out and funky. I took a nice hot bubble bath and then went back to sleep for another two hours. Once I got back up, I grabbed the napkin that was sitting on the dresser. Believe it or not, I was intrigued, and the way Taye had been acting, he was making it easy for a bitch to test the waters. Although good dick was hard to give up, I wasn't against finding more. Not that I was looking, but maybe it was time I started to.

Now feeling rejuvenated, I grabbed my phone and dialed the digits to call Batman. Of course I didn't get an answer, so at that point, I went downstairs and made me something to eat. I was in the mood for chicken and waffles, but since the chicken was frozen, I whipped up waffles and bacon. Kosh was in the living room doing something on her laptop. Usually, she would have hair to do since she was a stylist, but I guess she was taking the day off.

"Kosh, you sure you don't want any of this?"

"No, babe! I'm good!"

"Okay!"

I sat down once my food was done and started pigging out. As my phone sat on the table, it started buzzing. I noticed it was the number I dialed. Batman was calling me back. I answered, putting him on speaker.

"Hello."

"Is this the beautiful cat woman's voice I been waiting to hear?"

"You've been waiting? Oh, I got it like that already?"

"Oh, it's like that!"

I smiled and bit my lip. I was so curious as to who he was. I wanted to see his face.

"So, I have to say, I think it's unfair that you know what I look like, yet I have no clue what you really look like."

"That can be fixed real easily."

"What's your name?"

"It's me, Gold." Now his voice sounded familiar, unlike before. "It's Will." I started coughing, damn near choking on my food. "Gold, you alright?"

"Hold on." I had to grab something to drink. I never saw that coming. Kosh heard all my coughing and came running in the kitchen.

"Girl! You okay! Do I need to put your arms up?" she asked, alarmed as her eyes shot at me with uncertainty. "Shit, I can't do any other techniques to save your ass." Now my coughing turned to strained laughs. Will was laughing too since he was on speaker. That made Kosha jump since she didn't realize I had someone on the phone. "Oops, my bad! I didn't know you were talking to someone."

I finally was able to talk with my voice sounding a little strained from my windpipe being constricted.

"I'm okay. Thanks for checking on me though."

"Yeah, thank you, whoever you are," said Will.

Kosha mouthed, "Who's that... Batman?"

I just nodded my head yes. I figured I'd tell her about the man behind the costume later.

"You're welcome, Batman," she happily replied. She leaned in to speak closer to my phone. "It's Kosha! The one you gave the number to give to my girl here."

"Yeah. Oh! Okay. Thanks for doing that for me."

"You're welcome! I'll let you guys get back to it."

She had the biggest cheese on her face. She even gave a few quick claps before she left out the kitchen.

"Hello," said Will.

"I'm still here."

"You sure you're okay?"

"Fuck no! I ain't okay!" My attitude changed quick. "I knew you seemed familiar. I asked you if I knew you, and you told me no. Motherfucka, you lied to me."

"I didn't lie. The man I am now, Gold, you don't know. I was so surprised when I saw you at that party. I wanted to tell you who I was, but I panicked. You just looked so beautiful and I wanted to just hold you. I thought you was gon' figure it out and go crazy on me, so when you wanted me to say something, I changed my voice up, hoping to throw you off.

"Well, it worked, and it was a good thing you did because

I would've snapped on your ass. What the fuck you want, Will?"

I was heated.

"I know this was a shitty thing I did to get to you, and to this day, I regret our shit from the past. I'm sorry, Gold. My hope is that you'll give me another chance to show you I'm not like that boy I was before. My hope is that you'll let me take you out and show you who I am now."

"Whoa! How do you even know I'm not involved with someone?"

"I don't. All I know is that when I saw you, man... I wasn't letting you leave without me getting in ya presence. *Are you* seeing someone?"

All I thought while speaking to him was that he had a lot of balls.

"I'm keeping my options open... but for you—"

"Don't even say it. I just wanna know is it okay if I take you to dinner?"

"Will, I honestly don't even know how I feel about talking to you right now. I can't think about you without the thought of our baby. I don't think you understand how that shit fucks with me. The fact that you didn't want it and then shortly after didn't want me, hurt like hell! You were my first real love, but you didn't give a shit."

"I did, Gold. I just was young and immature, man. I didn't know having that abortion was a problem for you. On the

real, I didn't think you cared that much since you agreed
to it."

"Bullshit! You sat there and let yo' momma basically tell
us what to do, and you stood there and didn't say shit, but
you knew I wanted it."

"So you still blame me for it, and I can't change your
mind about me. Is that what you saying?"

"I don't know, Will, but as you can see, I still carry that
around me with. I honestly didn't realize how much it really
affected me until talking to you at this very moment."

"All I can say is, I'm sorry. I was young and stupid. I didn't
know what I wanted back then but I don't blame you for
being angry with me. Let me give you better memories of me,
Gold. Give me a chance. Just have dinner with me. Please?
That's all I'm asking." he concluded.

For some reason, I wanted to see him out of that costume,
and if nothing else, I'd be getting a meal I wasn't paying for.

"When, Will?"

"Next Sunday. I'm only saying then because that's when
I'll be completely available."

"Completely available, meaning?"

"Oh, I'll have more free time to spend here."

"What brought you this way in the first place?"

"One of my boys lives here. He getting married soon, so I
been back and forth for different things, getting ready. The
wedding's next Saturday, but they been having things
planned for us to do all week, leading up to that day. Man,"

he stressed, "the whole wedding party was at the Halloween party."

"Really? That's different."

"We had another one to hit up that night. His fiancée's idea. That's why I had to go so suddenly, since they were ready to go to the next one. I was mad too, especially once I knew you were there."

"I'm telling you now, Will, just because I go to dinner with you doesn't change my feelings about you."

"I understand, but I am sorry, Golden. I know that's not going to make up for anything, and you got your mind made up about me, but that's okay. I just want us to catch up as friends... if I can try to be your friend."

I had to admit, before I knew who he was, he had me interested. That *was* before, but I was willing to catch up with him, so I was going to take him up on his offer.

"I'll have dinner with you."

"Cool! I'll be in touch. I gotta head home to take care of some things for my mom, but I'll be back this way for the week."

"Okay."

"I'mma be staying at the *Troposphere Hotel,* so I'mma hit you up once I get back, if that's okay."

"It's fine."

"Alright! Well, you enjoy the rest of your day, and I look forward to getting reacquainted, *friend.*"

"Whatever! Bye, Will." I hung up. I felt let down now,

knowing it was him. Why should I expect prince charming anyway? Nothing in my life ever turned out like a fairytale. The next thing I knew, Kosha was back, standing in the archway, eyeing me for details. "Don't even look at me like that. It's not what you think at all."

"So you can read minds now?" She came and had a seat at the table with me. "So when are you two seeing each other again?"

"Hold your horses."

I explained to her who Batman was and a little bit about our history. Her being team anybody but Bronte, she was all for me still going to dinner with Will and giving him another chance. I told her I was still going with him, but the one thing I was not going to do was give him another chance. That ship had sailed.

5

NOVEMBER 13, 2005

I swear it seemed like Bronte had a radar for when a man was sniffing around me. He called me right after I spoke with Will and apologized for driving off like he did. I let it slide because I was snooping in his phone. Now I felt guilty for having this dinner date planned with Will, since I'd been hanging back with Bronte. He had been acting really weird these past couple of days; it was scary.

Kosha had been at the shop most of the week, and she worked long hours anyway, so my whereabouts weren't being questioned by her, luckily. And even though it was Sunday, she went in to the shop to do somebody's braids, so I knew she would have been gone most of today. But I had been over Taye's mostly, and it had been great! We hadn't argued or fought not once. Things for the most part were real chill.

I didn't even want to pull myself away to go on this date,

or dinner I should say, but my plan was to see Will and then just say goodbye. He had been calling and texting me throughout the week, and it wasn't easy responding. But I answered him whenever Bronte had left out, which wasn't much, or when I went back to Kosha's at night. I didn't even put much effort into getting ready, because I didn't want him to become suspicious and start asking questions since I hadn't got dolled up most of the week.

Of course, he had no clue I had been talking to Will or knew anything about Will. I had never discussed Will, with anyone, except for when I told Kosha about us, and I never gave her the full story. Nonetheless, I was meeting up with him, using my car that Taye got for me. He was so into his own shit he wasn't even worried about what I had going on anyway. He gave me a kiss and left out the house. Once I knew he was gone, I called Will.

"Hey! Sorry I missed your calls. I was busy earlier and couldn't talk, but since you want us to meet up sooner, yes, now is perfect."

"You sure? I don't wanna be an interruption if you wanna wait and keep it at six p.m. That's just in another two hours."

"No, now is fine."

"Well I'll be waiting at the bar in the restaurant."

"*Troposphere Hotel,* right?"

"Yeah. You sure you don't mind eating here? I just figured since the food is good it would be a great spot, but if you had somewhere else in mind, I would be down for it."

"There is fine, Will. I'm on my way."

I was glad he wanted it to be earlier, that way I could be gone right after Bronte left and hopefully back before he returned. The moment I arrived, I spotted Will immediately, waiting at the bar. I'm sure my mouth was hanging the whole time as I walked over to him. I knew it was, because the minute he noticed me, my cheeks automatically shifted to a smile with ease.

He stood to his feet and gave me a tight hug. Strangely, it didn't have the same effect it had on me when I didn't know who he was, but he really did look handsome. I got to see the fullness of his face, and even though he had facial hair, which didn't look this noticeable before, he still had his boyish looks. His haircut was nice and fresh, and his hairline was tight as fuck. He had the biggest grin on his face too when I pulled myself away and got to stare at him even more.

"Yo! You fine as fuck, ma."

"Stop it!" I urged.

I was dressed so casually; I wasn't even trying to impress him. I had on a pair of close fitted denim jeans, a pair of Ugg's, and a cream-colored top that ran partially up my neck, accompanied with a corduroy jacket that matched my boots. Even still, this nigga had me blushing like a dumbass.

"Come on. Let's sit at a table."

He took my hand and led the way. Part of me was nervous about that. I was scanning the room making sure I did *not* recognize *anybody* that knew Bronte. I knew I was being foolish, considering where this place was, but I didn't want no bullshit stirred up, especially since things were going so well with us. *Nothing wrong with being cautious*, I thought. It seemed the coast was clear, so I put my fears out of my mind and kept it moving. We found a table and took our seats. He even pulled the chair out for me.

"Look at you being a gentleman now," I joked.

"I told you, girl, you don't know me anymore."

"From the looks of you, you're right, but I can't vouch for anything else."

There was a twinkle in his eyes as he peered back at me.

"Aye, that's cool. You *damn* sure have changed, and you still single?" he asked, genuinely surprised. His eyes clung to me happily, awaiting my response. I felt kinda bad knowing I was about to douse his hopes of anything. I never let on that I had a man during our other conversations or texting.

"I'm not completely single."

His smile was still there but not as glowing.

"What's that supposed to mean?"

"Hello, guys, I'm Natalie, and I'll be serving you this evening. Would you like to start off with some drinks?" she offered as she set menus in front of us. "If you like I can give you two a moment to look it over and come back."

Will looked at me waiting to see what I wanted to do.

"Yeah, that would be nice," I told her.

"No problem! I'll be back shortly."

"Thank you," Will replied graciously.

I started looking over the menu, but of course Will was staring at me, likely waiting for me to explain saying I wasn't completely single. I shook my head while smiling before I looked at him since I could feel his eyes burning into me.

"What?"

"Don't what me. You got amnesia now?"

"No."

"So, what's changed within a few weeks? You got a man now, or don't you?" I swear as I gazed at that man's face, all I could think about was what our baby would have looked like. Would it have had my cocoa colored skin or his lightness? My big slanted eyes or his sunken shaped ones? "Gold! You okay?"

I wasn't okay as I sat there with him. It became more and more painful to be in his presence without thinking about our past, and I couldn't figure out why. It wasn't like I wanted him. I was over him and what we had. Plus, I loved Bronte, but something in me just wouldn't let the past go with Will. I placed the menu down. My whole demeanor had changed and set a brand-new tone. I took a good look at Will.

"Why did you let me go get that abortion by myself? Why didn't you want to be there for me?"

I knew he didn't want to have this discussion, but I needed to know. What surprised me was the fact that he responded right away.

"I'm about to tell you something that you didn't know. I may not have been in the waiting area in the building with you, but I was there. I sat outside in my boy Derrick's car. He let me borrow it. When you called, I made it seem like it had taken me a while to come get you, but I was there all along. My mom didn't even see me in the parking lot once she left, I guess after you were in recovery."

A tear ran down my face suddenly. It felt like I was in that head space all over again. His mother was only there because she had to be since I wasn't eighteen. The minute she knew the procedure was done she told the receptionist that I was to call Will and he would get me home because she had to go to work. That was the message I got from a nurse.

"You never stood up for me when it came to your mom. Were you that afraid to let her know you wanted to be there? Or did you want the baby too?"

Once he saw how emotional I was becoming, he no longer looked comfortable sitting there. He stood up and walked over to me.

"How 'bout we go up and order the food from the room and just finish this discussion up there? You seem to have a lot you wanna get off ya chest with this, and you deserve your questions answered. Please, Golden," he suggested as he gazed at me with sincerity. "We shouldn't discuss this here." He was right, so I stood with him. "Are you still going to be able to eat something?"

"I don't know... maybe," I added as I wiped my face.

"I'mma go find Natalie and let her know what's up. I'll be right back."

My left hand instantly held onto my right arm as I waited for him to return. Once he did, we left the restaurant that was connected to the hotel and took the elevator to his room. It had just occurred to me that I had no clue what Will did for a living. We were in a five-star hotel, and once we got to his room, it was huge and gorgeous. He had an incredible view overlooking the water. It had a kitchen, a bar, and a nice office area. The glamour of it all had started to ease my mind.

"This room is amazing! It's so beautiful."

"Yeah, I'm only in here because we had it for the guys to stay in, from the wedding. Everybody else has headed out but I decided to stay a few more days, so I just kept this room."

"Damn! You balling!"

He rubbed his hands together with a smile.

"I've been fortunate. Have a seat though." He sat beside me on the couch. "Before we start talking. Do you want to order some food? That way it could be on the way sooner rather than later or..."

"You're hungry, aren't you?"

He laughed.

"Yo! I ain't gon' lie. My ass is starving," he said with laughter again afterwards.

"Sure."

We got that out of the way, and then he got serious, as did I. He took my hand as we sat together.

"Gold, look. I did agree with my mom about us being

young and not having shit to give a child. I wasn't ready for that kind of responsibility. On the other hand, I shouldn't have let that excuse the fact that I should've been there with you instead of making you feel like I didn't really care."

"Be honest, Will! You didn't care, because right after that, you left me. Then I found out you were cheating on me, telling whoever that bitch was I was your best friend." I yanked my hand away and pushed him. "How could you do that to me? I fuckin' loved you! You were all I had."

He heavily sighed.

"Look, I can't do nothing about that shit now. I don't know how many times or ways I can tell you I'm sorry. But ya crazy ass got me back for that shit anyway." He started pointing at me. "Yeah, I know what you did."

I rolled my eyes at him and turned my head in the other direction.

"I didn't do nothing!"

"Yes, you did, but I don't hold it against you."

I turned my head and stared at him again with my brows snapped together.

"I didn't do anything!"

His eyebrows lifted in disbelief, and his eyes widened at my audacity.

"Gold, you fucked my shit up. I had to get a new ride because of yo' ass."

"That wasn't me! I don't know what you talking about."

"Then the girl told me you came after her. I know for a

fact that was you that fought her. Shit! She even said it was you."

"That bitch looked like she stayed with enemies. Anybody could've whipped her tricking ass."

"I still can't believe you sitting up here denying it, man. Everybody that lived on the block was talking about it, and they also said it was you. *You* fucked up my car and beat ol' girl's ass. I didn't even get to enjoy having it for long." I busted out laughing. I refused to admit shit, but I remembered that day like yesterday, and the thought of that shit was so gratifying. "That's why you laughing," he observed, grinning at me.

"No, it's not. I'm laughing because I remember hearing how bad your car looked. They said ya windows was completely shattered, the car was keyed up and spray painted bad, and all ya tires were flat as pancakes. Somebody got you good, boo, but it wasn't me," I denied, looking straight ahead.

"Yo! I'mma let you have that because I know I did you wrong, and I'm sorry for that shit. For real. Look at me." I rolled my eyes first like I didn't want to look at him. Then I did as he asked. "I'm really not that dude no more, Gold. I've matured a lot, man. I'm working all the time, traveling, and just enjoying life. No kids or steady woman yet. I'm starting to think me getting to this moment here is the reason for that."

I had to bring things back to reality for him.

"Um... Will... the reason why I told you that I wasn't completely single was because I've been off and on with my man. We had a fight when I bumped into you last. At the Halloween party," I reminded. "I had no idea what I wanted then, and then finding out who you turned out to be, I honestly have no intentions of anything transpiring between us again. I'm sorry."

We were saved from anymore awkwardness since our food had been delivered. Will got up and received the entrees. He placed them on the table, got more napkins for us, and took a bottle of red wine out too.

"You still drink red wine, right?"

"I do!"

Will had ordered a thick, juicy steak with a stuffed sweet potato and spinach with mushrooms and onions. I ordered the rotisserie chicken, with mashed potatoes, and broccoli. My thought was to get something I knew Bronte would like if I didn't eat it all. I would just tell him Kosha got it for me if he asked. He put my drink down beside me and took his seat. I saw him bow his head and say a quick prayer before he dug in. Who was this man?

"Will, what do you do for a living? You never said."

"Oh, I'mma web designer."

"Really? I never would've guessed."

He sat his fork down and looked me in the eyes with a straight face.

"Look, I know you said what you said about things. I just

hope whoever you with is treating you right and appreciating what he has since you've given him another chance."

"Believe me, it's not like that. He does love me and takes very good care of me. I don't have to ask for nothing. Everything was just a big misunderstanding."

"I'm sorry that's all it was. We had some good times together. Didn't we?"

"We did," I agreed, grinning.

"Remember when we were alone at the crib, and it was hot in that bitch because the air was broke?" he mentioned with a chuckle.

I smiled so wide because that was a great memory of us...

Hmm... I wonder what he's holding, I thought.

"Will, it's your turn."

"I know. Lemme get comfortable real quick."

He took his beater off that he was wearing but left his basketball shorts on. He knew I loved his chest. He thought he was going to distract me.

"Can you hurry up?"

"Alright! I'm ready." I noticed he had four cards left, and I still had all seven of mine. He dropped three. "Uno!"

"Ooo, you sneak! Okay... so the color is yellow? Well, how you like this?" I bragged as I changed it. I dropped a blue eight over his yellow eight. I had nothing! Couldn't make him draw two or four. All my hope was on that being the game changer and keeping him in it. I anxiously watched his hand as he prepared to either pluck or go out of the game. He knew I was eager to see and stalled.

"Damn, man!" He complained and plucked.

I got excited and threw my arms in the air as I sat Indian style across from him on his bed. I almost messed up the deck.

"Yes!"

"Will you just go," he demanded with a smile.

"Do I detect some animosity?" I asked as I plucked. Then I shook my shoulders and did my little happy dance, glad that he didn't go out. I put down a blue two. Will didn't pluck again. He put down a wild card.

"Uno! The color is yellow." I threw my cards down since I knew I lost. "What'd you do that for?"

"Your last card is yellow. I don't have anything to stop you, so it's over."

"It didn't have to be."

I looked at him confused. He showed me his card. He had a draw four in his hand which meant he never had to pluck in the first place. This game should have been over, but he was extending it. I jumped up and dove on him, making him fall back.

"Aw you were playing, so I could win?" I asked sweetly.

"Nooo. I just wanted to punish you a little longer. Make you sweat."

He was going to get it for that. We got to wrestling on the bed. I was trying to get him in a choke hold since I was on top of him, but he flipped me over.

"You can't see me, so don't even try."

I laid there, tired and out of breath.

"Will, why is it so hot in here? The wallpaper is even peeling from the walls." I joked.

He laughed at me.

"I thought I told you my mom said we having problems with the air."

"You probably did, and I forgot but damn!"

"She s'posed to be getting somebody to look into it sometime today. You wanna go down in the basement instead? It's cooler."

"We can tough it out for the night I guess."

"I'll make sure to keep you nice and cool."

"By doing?"

I extended my leg and dragged my toes against his body.

"Take ya clothes off and I'll show you."

"How 'bout you take my clothes off."

"You ain't said nothing. Let me do a few things that'll help with reducing the temperature in this room first, but you know I can't speak for yours. You 'bout to have a fever."

"I already do. It's Will fever. I've had it for some time now."

He smiled and got off the bed. He turned on some music and lowered the volume. It was a mix of artists, but the first one on the CD was Sade. The lighting was dim, but he turned it off and made sure the curtains were pulled so the nighttime ambiance could spill in. Then he put his shirt and sports slippers back on and walked out of the room.

I was lying there with my arms and legs spread because I was hot, and I wanted my clothes off, but I wanted him to remove them. He came back with a cooler filled with ice, additional bottles *of water, and a pint of ice cream with a miniature scooper. He set it down on the nightstand and removed his shirt again.*

"I like the way you're thinking."

"'Cause daddy knows just what you like."

"Daddy, can you pass me one of the water bottles please?"

He threw it to me.

"Catch!"

Of course, I didn't catch it, but it still landed on the bed. Will handed it to me. I started taking a few gulps and then set it back on the nightstand on my side. Will started removing the cards off the bed since we had them scattered everywhere. I was sitting on some of them. His eyes strolled to my ass. My cue to lift. I leaned over on my side so he could grab the ones I was on. I should have sat there and let his hand feel its way to find them. Once he got them all, he put them up. From that moment on, his focus was solely on me.

"Lay back," *he commanded. I did just that. He took his time inching my shorts off.* "You feeling alright?" *I bit on the tip of my nail as I watched him and nodded my head yes.* "Just lay back and relax, okay?"

"That's not going to be easy," *I murmured.*

I was anxious for him especially since he was massaging my right foot, thoroughly.

"Don't worry, baby, I got you. Now how that feel?"

My eyes had closed, and I just relaxed and enjoyed his touch. I didn't even want to respond. I just wanted him to see my face to know. He put that foot down and worked on the other one. His hands were making me feel like putty. He could've molded me any way he liked, and it would've been alright.

Once he was done with that one, he climbed up to me and took me out of my short-sleeved shirt. My bra was already unhooked from earlier since I was hot. I needed these girls to breathe. He nicely slid the straps off my arms and tossed the bra.

"Lay on your stomach."

Without hesitation, I turned over and let my head rest on my arms. Will reached his arm out and grabbed something out of the cooler that was sitting on the nightstand on his side. The next thing I felt was drops of cold water. I squirmed from the sudden cool shock, and unexpectedly, I shouted.

"Ahhh!"

He noticed my reaction as I felt it on my neck and then my backbones. Next, the trail traveled down my spine.

"This will take the edge off."

His warm tongue licked each spot where the droplets of water landed and sopped up what was on my moistened skin. Each lick made my toes curl and my body jerk, causing my ass to poke out. Next, his deep sultry voice whispered in my ear.

"You like that, baby?"

"Mmm, babe, I do," I uttered, faintly.

He planted a kiss on my lips before pulling my panties completely off.

"Turn over." I gladly changed positions again and got on my back. Will grabbed for the ice cream that was softening. "You ready for this?"

Softy, I responded.

"I'm ready."

He took the miniature scooper that was sitting in the cooler and dipped some out, to feed to me first. It was Vanilla. Then he tasted the remnants from my lips. He was sweating up a storm as he hovered over me. Since I knew he was hot I took a few pieces of ice out of the cooler and rubbed it on his chest. I started with each nipple. His firm body tightened from the cold sensation.

I took a bigger piece out and slowly glided it down his broad shoulders and muscular arms. I could see he was feeling good. Then I put another piece of ice in my mouth, lifted my body up some and attempted to roll it over his face with my teeth, but it got too cold and I dropped it on myself making both of us laugh. But Will gladly ate it up.

He was ready to put the attention back on me. He kissed my belly before he took his tongue and drilled it into my navel along its travels. "Mmm..." I moaned. He didn't stop there. His lips continued making their way down to my parted lips and gave them the juiciest kisses. "Ahhh..." I squealed as I grabbed his head to release my sexual tension. I was ready to explode.

His French kisses had my legs trembling, but then he stopped. With the ice cream scooper still in hand he filled it with more of the ice cream and dropped a dollop on each nipple along with my pussy. You talk about pleasure and pain. I screamed as my body cringed.

"Will, lick it!" *I yelled.* "Ooo please!" *I begged.* "Please, baby!"

He devoured his dessert in all three places. I continuously rubbed my foot down his leg as he viciously consumed me. My pussy was so wet from him... for him too. My skin may have felt cooled, but I was in heat. After that, Will finally pulled down his shorts and boxers and used his knees to spread my legs wider. My boo entered me nice and slow. I tugged on the sheets from the exhilaration his pole was giving me.

He leaned into me and shifted on his side. Then he took my right leg and wrapped it over him and used my ass to bring me closer to him as he stroked. We grinded and kissed as I ran my hands all through his waved hair. I pulled away just to moan because he was putting this pussy to bed. Nighty night! Our bodies generated so much more heat leaving us sweaty on the outside but cool as ice in our own world on the inside. Even still, I was melting away.

"Ah! Ah! Ah!"

Was all I could get out. Each pitch sounding higher than before. His loving felt so good. I had experienced nothing like it. He was my first real love.

"Go 'head and buss, baby... come on... cum fo' daddy."

I'm cumming for daddy. Daddy is... about to... get a special delivery..." I sang. "Sooner than I would've liked. Ahhhh!" I screamed from my release.

That was it. The sound of monumental bliss. No longer could I hold on. In my mind, although it felt sooo good, I was mad as hell that I had cum so soon. His loving was just that damn good. I laid there looking at the ceiling, wanting my body to settle down so we could do it again, and maybe the second time I would last. Will had put his arm under my head and pushed me over to cuddle with him.

"I thought I was going to be in your arms forever. We had a lot of good times together," I stated as my smile diminished. "That's why it hurt so bad when I found out you had been cheating on me and didn't want me anymore."

"You're never going to forgive me, are you?"

"I don't even know how to forgive myself."

"You need to, Gold. That was so many years ago."

I didn't say anything, because no matter how long ago it was, I honestly didn't know how to forgive myself for the abortion. As shitty as my childhood was, it never stopped me from wanting to someday have a family of my own.

"I better get going before it gets too late."

I got up and took a quick sip of what was left in my wine glass before I gathered up my food to trash it, which was practically nothing. That food was amazing. I tore that meal up as we reminisced.

"Is it okay if I see you to your car?"

Soon as he said that, my phone started ringing. It was Bronte. I became frantic since I knew I needed to answer.

"Oh, I need to take this." I scurried to the door. "You don't need to walk me. I'll be fine."

Just like Will, he had quickly followed behind me, grabbing on my arm, looking concerned.

"Yo! Slow down. You okay?"

I needed him to let me leave. I could not talk to Taye with

Will standing there. I also didn't want to miss his call and he get suspicious. I yanked my arm away from him.

"I'm great! I just need to go! Thanks for dinner."

I opened the door and ran to the car that was parked outside the restaurant. Once I got in, I called Bronte back since I ended up missing his call. I tried to hide the fact that I was out of breath as we spoke, because I sure as hell was tired from running.

"Hey, babe! What's up?"

"Where you at?"

"I'm driving, on my way back there. You home?"

"Yeah, I'm here. Didn't know you were leaving though."

"Yeah... I'd... uh, needed to run to Kosh's for a bit. You need anything before I get there?"

"No, I'm straight. I do need to talk to you though, so I'll see you when you get here. Hurry up!"

"Alright, babe."

When I got in, I noticed my phone buzzing. The minute I looked at it, Bronte was headed in my direction. I saw it was Will and hurried up and forwarded it. Bronte was so happy to see me it blew me away.

"Mmm, I missed you," he gushed as he embraced me closely, holding his hands in his favorite spot.

"I missed you too, babe." He kissed me, and as he did, I felt my phone going off again. Bronte pulled his lips away. "Who's that?"

I had to think fast.

"It's not you calling, so I don't care who it is, but it's probably Kosha."

"She act like ya nigga the way she be blowing you up and shit. Didn't you just leave her hoe ass?"

Bronte let me go and went to sit on the couch and grabbed the remote. I didn't even respond to that. I just let it go. I noticed the TV was on showing a basketball game. I guess that was what he was doing before I came in. He loved sports, and when games were on, that usually had his attention sometimes more than me.

"I'm going to get comfortable and then I'll be back down here."

"Alright, babe."

I went to sneak and text Will back so he could stop calling and texting me. He would not let up and told me he wouldn't stop until he heard my voice to know I was okay. I had to call him. I hit the phone icon in his chat and called him and spoke at a whisper.

"Hey! Will! I'm fine!"

"Yo! Why you run off like that, man? You didn't e—"

"Will, I have to go! You said you wanted to hear my voice. Well you just heard it. I'm okay."

"Then why you whispering?"

I checked in the hallway to make sure Bronte wasn't in sight and still downstairs.

"Because I do have a man that would think something if he heard me on the phone with you. Now I gotta go! Please don't call me back or text me anymore tonight. I'm going to be here, so I'm about to shut off my phone."

"Okay! Wait! I promise not to call you no more tonight, but do me favor."

"What, Will? I told you I gotta go!"

"Can you just call me when you have some time alone? I just wanna ask you a few things, and then I'll leave you alone. I promise."

"Okay. Goodbye, Will."

I loudly sighed after I hung up that call.

"What's wrong?"

I didn't even hear his ass coming up the stairs, yet here he was walking in the bedroom. Damn, he was good at that shit, which was why I peeked not too long ago.

"Oh! I'm... I'm just tired is all," I stammered, getting out.

"You see the DVD remote? I was gonna put something on."

"It's probably down in one of the cushions. I'm sorry, babe. I had it last and must've sat it on the couch instead of putting it on the entertainment stand."

"I thought you were going to get comfortable. Why you still ain't undressed."

My heart rate gradually increased. I knew I had to settle myself because if I didn't, it would have gotten him suspicious. I didn't want that, especially since things had been so well between us.

"Kosha," I said, shaking my head. "I was talking to her and hadn't had a chance to undress yet." I headed to the dresser. "I'm going to get comfortable right now," I assured him.

"Alright, I'll try to grab the remote. You want any wine or anything."

I looked back at him with my hands clasped together.

"Babe, that would be great!"

"Alright, and remind that hoe who ya man is."

"Be nice!"

I got my feet massaged while we just chilled and watched a movie. We never did talk, which was a conversation I damn sure was curious about having, but I decided I was going to wait and let him bring it up. I was always left waiting for him to bring what he wanted to talk about up before I had to break down and ask.

THE NEXT MORNING, I was served breakfast in bed. I swear I didn't know what had got into Bronte, but I was loving it. He was being so attentive to me. We spent the whole day together, just enjoying each other, and when it was time for dinner later, he decided to grill.

While I was up in the bedroom fixing my hair, I was on the phone getting cussed out by Kosha. She was mad at me for being with Bronte, after she knew I had a date with Will. I said fuck it and told her I was at his house. That conversation didn't end well.

Once we hung up, I walked out in the yard to see what Taye had been doing and noticed he was out there with some steaks on the grill. I also noticed a colorful tossed salad in a bowl, covered. It looked like some corn was grilling too. I sat down on the lawn furniture and watched him tend to the meat.

"This pretty, ain't it?" he asked, holding up the steak showing me the grill marks.

"Looking good," I humorously replied.

"So, what's up witchu?" he asked as he took a seat beside me.

"Nothing."

"Don't seem like it's nothing to me."

"I thought you wanted to talk, Bronte."

Kosha nicely reminded me of the reason I told her why I was here, since I said we hadn't talked yet. I lied and told her that was the only reason I was here.

"Alright, man! It's like this. I'm sorry for the way I've acted towards you in the past and taking you for granted. I know I been mad crazy and tripping 'bout shit, and I'm sorry. I shouldn't be thinking just because I fucked up, that you already did me the same way."

"What about when you get mad, Bronte, and let your temper get the best of you? I'm tired of us fighting and you talking crazy to me."

"Don't sit up and here and act like you didn't know who I was before you started messing with me. Some things may have changed, but you right; not everything. Then you go and call the fuckin' cops on me. You don't know how bad that shit fucked my head up."

"Believe me. You showed it. I knew! But that was after I got tired of your behavior and fed up with the bullshit. I've apologized to you hundreds of times. You got to know I love you, Bronte, and that's something I'll never do again."

"I know. That's why all the bullshit gon' stop."

"You mean it?"

"Every word, and I'mma start showing you too, and loosening the reins a little more, letting you see that I trust you."

"Why should I believe you this time?"

"You don't have to do shit. All you can do is take my word and see."

He put his hand out, and I grabbed it while getting up. I sat on his lap. He wrapped his arms around me.

"Baby, I'm sorry for hurting you, and I'mma do my best to be the man you first met."

"Did you fuck those girls that's been calling ya phone, Taye?"

He frowned up like it was a preposterous question.

"Who?"

"You know who I'm talking about. Did you? Tell me the truth."

"I'm not even gon' answer that. All that shit is in the past."

"So that's a yes," I concluded, feeling validated.

"Why we even talking 'bout them? I got who I wanna fuck *always,* right here." Then he cupped my pussy. "You ain't give my shit away since we been apart, have you?"

"Don't think I didn't notice how you're trying to change the subject, but no."

"You know this gon' always be mine, right?" he said, giving it a few rubs. I didn't say anything. "Right?" he asked again, wanting an answer.

I responded with a smile.

"Right, Bronte. That's why I'm here."

"I got something for you."

He piqued my curiosity, making the smile I already had wider. He kissed me then patted my leg, letting me know he needed to get up to check on the food.

"Bronte, what is it?"

"Hold on. Let me feed you first." Once all the food was prepared, we had a very nice dinner out in the yard. We laughed, and not once did we argue. I went to take the dishes in the house. As I was putting them in the sink, Bronte crept up behind me, lifted his arm out alongside me, and smoothly presented an opened ring box in front of me. My mouth dropped as I stared at the beautiful huge diamond. He moved his hand from my side so I could turn to face him, then held it back in front of me.

"I love you, baby. Will you marry me?"

I smacked his shoulder because I was so emotional. I didn't know how to take him.

"Bronte, don't you fuckin' be playing with me, Bronte." I started crying, hitting him more in his chest. "Don't play with me!"

He grabbed me by my arms.

"Babe, I'm not playing," he confirmed with a smile. "Stop tripping! I'm serious."

I cried some more as I shook my head yes while he put the ring on my finger. I hugged him around the neck from being so happy. He picked me up and spun me around. I never imagined us getting married, but I was so happy about it. He took my hand and led me up to his room to celebrate. I swear he knew how to keep me falling for him. He always convinced me of how much he loved me, even more when we were in the bedroom.

He was on top, making love to me. I had my legs spread, but my feet were clasped around his calves. My hands cupped his ass, and I was squeezing my pussy all on his pole as he stroked me relentlessly. We had that bed rocking. I loved having his plug in my socket. Talk about electricity. He was hitting it so good he had me ignited, moaning extra loud, when suddenly his doorbell rang. His movement stopped. I noticed he had this strange look on his face.

"Babe, who's that?"

"... I don't know, but they'll leave," he finally managed to say.

He went back to fucking me. The bell chimed again. He didn't stop this time. He kept on stroking, and I kept grinding till I couldn't take the noise anymore.

"Bronte! It doesn't seem like whoever it is, is going away. Who the fuck is that?"

He started kissing me, obviously to shut me up while he continued to stroke.

Ding Dong! Ding Dong! Ding Dong! Shit wouldn't stop.

"Fuck!" he hissed. "Stay right up here. I'll be back."

Fuck if I was staying right there. He had already gone to get the door. I wanted to see what all this urgency was, so I put on one of his shirts. As I was buttoning it, I heard a female's voice, and she was angry. I walked right down those steps, wanting to see this bitch. Bronte was in the doorway while she was standing outside. He was telling her to leave. Apparently, she was mad at him because I was there. How she knew that, I had no clue, but this bitch was about to really know about Golden.

"Is there a problem here?" I inquired cockily. I was on my tippy toes, peeking over Bronte's shoulder, since he was blocking the door.

"Gold, go back upstairs. I got this."

"So, you back wit' her now?" the chick asked. Then she looked at me, annoyed since I didn't move. "Hope you know he's been all up in this pussy, bitch!"

"Bitch?"

My hand went beside Bronte's arm so fast as I mushed

that bitch in her face. He had to pry my hand away since my grip was so tight. I wanted my imprint left on her fuckin' skin. I got with her ugly ass the best I could. When Bronte finally pulled my hand away, my nail markings showed all on her face.

I didn't know who the fuck she thought I was, but I bet she knew now. She still was trying to fight me, but Bronte shoved her out the way as he tried to get her to just leave. I couldn't see why he was trying to reason with her in the first place. She should've been introduced to the door the second he saw who it was.

"Yo! Get the fuck away from my house with dat nonsense, man. Not having this shit! Go!" He spat while he shooed her ass on then shut his door on her.

She was still out there talking trash outside the door. I wanted to come out there so badly and give her some hands for real, but he kept holding me back till she finally left. I stomped my way upstairs to start getting dressed. Bronte followed me to the room and stood in his doorway.

"I hope you don't believe that girl."

I stopped unbuttoning his shirt I had on for a second.

"I do believe her," I retorted with my hand on my hip. "She was way too upset to be lying."

"That was the point. Gold, I swear I didn't fuck that girl."

"And why should I believe you? You've cheated on me before and lied about it, when to this day, I know I would've never found out if your butt hadn't dialed my number, and I

—" I shook my head at the thought. "I'm not even going to get into that. Just know that was one of the worst days of my life."

"How long you gon' make me pay for that when you know I'm trying? And why you so quick to believe other people over me?"

"Need you ask!" I refuted, flaring my arms.

"Why da fuck you hollering?"

"Because this is what you make me do!"

I was back to taking that shirt off and then getting my clothes to put on.

"Look, we were just fine before she came here causing shit. Can you stop getting dressed and just talk to me without yelling?"

I had just found my bra. I sat on the bed putting it on when Bronte threw his body on top of me, making me fall back. I was so upset because I loved him so much, but sometimes he treated me like shit, but always claimed to love me. I thought he really meant what he said, especially since he proposed, but now I wasn't so sure anymore.

"Move, Bronte! I'm not playing!"

"Nah, you not leaving."

"I don't even know why I believed you then. All you do is lie to me."

"I'm not lying this time. She is! Just for you to get mad like you are now and letting her win."

"What is she doing just coming over here then?"

"Shit! I don't know. I didn't invite her ass over."

"But you have before, *obviously.*"

"Look, she did come over here once. We stayed in the living room the whole time. Nothing happened. She knew I wasn't fuckin' 'round, but she wanted to come chill, so I let her."

"You're such a liar. Just shut up!"

I squirmed around some more trying to get up, but he kept me pinned down.

"I'm serious. We chilled for a minute, and then I told her I had something to do."

"So, you invited a bitch over but didn't fuck her?"

"Yeah."

My hands broke free, and I kept hitting him continuously in his back.

"Move! I ain't fooling with you. You can't be trusted. I'm just wasting my time with you!"

He was so calm while he laid on me just holding my shoulders down. He didn't even react to my hitting him like that till I stopped.

"You really can't be mad at me doe. You left me, or did you forget that? Now all I'm doing is being honest witchu. You know them girls don't mean shit to me. Nobody else will ever mean as much to me as you do. Baby, I love *you!*" he stressed. "I asked *you* to marry me. Nobody else but you." He stroked my face as his eyes trailed over it. "You believe me, don't you?"

I really didn't know what to think. He was so good at lying to me and convincing me to see things his way. I wasn't sure if this was another attempt. I was confused.

"Yes... no... maybe. I don't know," I frustratedly admitted.

"Baby, believe me," he said sincerely.

"You're always making me promises, Taye, and never keeping them. Why can't you just be honest?"

He continued stroking my face and wiping the tears away that started to fall again.

"I am gon' be honest with you," he confessed. He laid his head on my chest. "I have so much love for you that I get afraid sometimes of losing ya love. I don't wanna lose you, baby," he declared, giving my shoulders an affectionate squeeze.

"Sometimes I don't think you really care about losing me. I think you always believe that I'm gonna end up coming back, since I always have."

He lifted his head up real quick to look at me.

"Nooo... no, baby. I don't feel that way at all. I just be talking shit, but I don't be meaning none of it. Without you, I have a lot to lose. Why you think I keep coming back too?"

"Then you need to change, Bronte, 'cause I don't know how much more of this I can take, and giving me this ring isn't going to stop me from leaving. Us fighting and you lying and cheating on me, although I could only prove it once, is not showing me that you really love me. I hope that's all out of your system."

"I know my actions haven't been the best, but baby, I love you more than anything, and I'm gon' spend the rest of our life proving it to you. I'm honestly ready to give you everything you want me to. Things gon' be different. I promise."

When he said that, I felt like I was right back in that moment when he first cheated on me and tried to apologize for that. I didn't want to ever relive that feeling, yet here it was, taking me back to that day. Even then, he wasn't expecting me to hear him blowing a bitch's back out over the phone, until he noticed I was on the call. He said hello and heard my voice. The next thing I knew, he was at my spot, and since he had a key, he let himself in.

"Golden, baby, wait!" I moved my ass away from him, but he continued to follow me as we circled my couch. "I'm sorry I hurt you. Just hear me out. I just wanna talk to you and explain."

"No! Get away from me, Bronte! Just leave!"

He slowly came toward me with his hands out to comfort me since I felt like I was dying on the inside. I cried hysterically from the hurt he caused. As he came forward, I moved away.

"I'm sorry! I'm so fuckin' sorry you had to hear that, and I hurt you, baby. I don't know what came over me. I fucked up! But that's why I'm here. I'm only here because I love you."

"Nooo! You don't... you... you... fucked herrr! You bastard!"

"Baby, you right! I did it, and I was wrong. I'm sorry. I'm so sorry! Please believe I'm sorry, Gold."

"No! I don't believe shit, okay! I just want you to leave me alone."

"I can't! I wanna make up to you all the hurt and pain I've caused you. I'm here to love you better, baby. Just let me."

"No! You had your chance and you blew it. I knew something was off, but I never could prove it. Time and time again, I trusted and believed that you were gonna change and really love me like I deserved. But I wasn't good enough. I just wasn't enough for you. Huh, Bronte! You just had to have more. Well, now you can, freely, okay! I can't do this with you anymore, so just go," I commanded, pointing.

He had this look like my words were tearing him to shreds. Like he really felt all the hurt and pain that I had been feeling for so long.

"Can't you see that I love you? I don't want another woman. I don't wanna touch another woman." He walked a little closer since I wouldn't allow him to come near me. "I only wanna have you in my arms... feel ya lips pressed up against mine... ya scent laying next to me... you're the only woman that I'll ever truly love... please, baby, believe me." I was confused. I wanted to hit him, but he looked so pitiful and serious. Then I saw tears falling from his eyes. That confused me even more. I was stuck. He softly spoke. "I love you so much... come on, baby... listen to me. I'mma change... I promise."

He inched a little closer and I allowed him too. Then he pulled me close. We were face to face. He gave me several small pecks on my lips. I didn't fully kiss him back right away, but who was I kidding. I still loved him. We had four years in by now, but I *remained strong and made him wait before I agreed to go back to him.*

He knew how to get to me ever since. He kissed me after making more promises of the same. I always wanted to believe him, and also believed he was who I deserved, so instead of me dressing to leave, I allowed him to undress me to pick up where we left off.

6

DECEMBER 1, 2005

I took my car and drove over to Kosh's to get some things. I was going to stay over Bronte's for a little while since previously, I had been coming home at night. She was entertaining some guy when I got in. They were sitting in the living room watching a movie.

"Hey! Oh! Hello," I also said while waving to her guest.

"How you doing?"

"Gold, this is Kevin."

"Well, I'll be in and out."

Kosha turned to her friend.

"Kev, can you excuse me for a second?"

"Yeah."

I was on my way up the stairs. Kosh was following right behind me. Once I turned on the light in the room, I gathered some things.

"Is asshole waiting outside?" She hassled since she noticed I wasn't staying.

"He is not an asshole; he is my fiancé." I bragged, lifting my hand in the air and displaying my ring. I hadn't shown it to her until now. She came close to me and held my hand and examined it.

"You have got to be kidding me. You're going to marry that sorry son of a bitch!"

I yanked my hand away and went to pull some things out of the dresser.

"I'm going back to Bronte's. I just came here to get a few things."

"Won't you live with him then, since you're marrying his trifling ass."

I swung my head around to look at her.

"Really, Kosh? You really want me to leave?"

"You're already gone!"

Now she had me angry and tight in my chest as I eyeballed her.

"What's that supposed to mean?"

"How many times are you going to let him put his cheating hands on you before you realize he ain't shit!"

I went back to packing my things and stuffing them in my duffle bag as l continued our exchange.

"I swear you exaggerate everything when it comes to Bronte, because you don't like him. Well, guess what? You don't have to like him. It's not expected of *you* to like him.

What is expected was you to just be my homegirl. That's all!"

"You're so blinded by him you can't even see that's what I'm being and have been is ya homegirl. But you go 'head back to him, and this time when he whips your ass over something as dumb as going out and enjoying yourself, don't come to me crying. This chick right here has had enough!"

"I'm sorry you feel that way, Kosha," I said as I faced her direction with lingerie in my hand.

"Oh! Don't let me see Bronte, because I'm going to tell him about you and Will. See how he feels about marrying dat ass then!"

I dropped the things I had in my hand and got in her face with the quickness.

"Stay the fuck out my business, Kosh!"

The one thing we had never done was fought each other, but I swear we were about to go to blows if she even thought she was going to ruin my shit.

"Get the fuck out my face, Golden. I'm telling you," she threatened.

I wasn't moving, and best believe my hands were ready, but because she was supposed to be my homegirl, I didn't leap.

"No! I'm telling you! Mind ya fuckin' business."

She shook her head with her lips puckered and eyes crinkled in the corners as she stared at me like I repulsed her.

"You's a dumb ass bitch."

Womp! Cracked her right in her fuckin' mouth. She grabbed that spot and realized her lip was bleeding. That was the beginning of us rumbling in the room. We were going at it, blow for blow, until her friend ran up the stairs and got in between us. He pulled Kosha away as we were huddled over each other punching and grabbing whatever we could.

"Yo! Yo!" he shouted as he was making his way between us. Kosh! Stop, y'all!"

He threw us in corners. We both were out of breath.

"Bitch, get ya shit and get the fuck outta here!" she yelled. He helped her up.

I was already gathering my stuff so what she was saying, wasn't a damn thing. Now, I just had to take it all. She turned around and walked out the room with her friend. I heard him telling her to come to the kitchen with him so she could get some ice on her lip.

I couldn't believe she threatened to tell Bronte I saw Will. What type of shit was that? Sadly, I knew which incident she was referring to about Bronte. I wished I never told her. We had gone out one night, and since I knew Kosha wasn't coming home, I let Bronte stay at her house till I came back. I had just been hanging over there and had spent a few nights with her. I still had my spot at the room share, but since we had been going out a lot and getting in late, I chilled at

Kosha's for a bit. This particular night, I had Bronte's car since I knew Kosh and I wouldn't have been returning together. I didn't make it in till three in the morning, and yes, I did have a nice time.

When I got in, Bronte was up, waiting on the couch in the living room with the television on. His forearms were resting on his legs as he leaned like he was engrossed in the TV. He was still fully clothed and everything. I walked over to him and stood on the side of him as he sat on the couch. Little did I know I was in for some drama.

"Baby, you been waiting up for me all this time. How sweet!" He slowly turned his head to the side with his eyes cut like I said something stupid. *"What's wrong?"* He grabbed my dress, pulling me down on the couch and leaned over on me.

"Fuck you doing comin' in here at this time when you knew I was here waitin'?"

"You wanted to be here. I didn't ask you to stay," I replied frantically.

"Exactly why you should've brought yo' ass home sooner." I was so sick of his controlling and possessive ways, which did it for me. I pushed him off me and got up. *"Fuck's wrong witchu, girl?"* he yelled.

"Get the fuck out! You're not going to be putting your hands on me, dammit!"

"I'm not going nowhere till I'm fuckin' ready," he snarled back.

"I want you out of here. It's over!"

"I don't give a fuck!"

"Then leave!" I yelled, pointing to the door.

"I'll leave when I'm damn ready to leave. Fuck is you? Whatchu gotta nigga all up in ya head feedin' you lies and bullshit too? You think he better than me now, so you got balls to tell me it's over? Is that it?" he said with a sudden adjust in attitude.

I walked over to the door and opened it.

"Get out!"

He stood there for a second, staring at me. Then he came over and looked down on me.

"I don't need ya ass anyway, but tell me somethin', Gold. Where da fuck would you be without me, huh? I make dat ass... you have nothin' without me... remember dat shit. I'm out!"

"Can I have my key back please?" I asked stern as he walked past.

"Fuck no!" He shouted, while he kept on walking.

He got in his car and drove off. I slammed the door. I was heated with him and really felt like this time I was done with him, so I thought.

She knew a lot when it came to me and Bronte. Now I regret her knowing so much. I was so done with her bullshit when it came to him. I got my things, made sure the room was tidy and back in the condition before I came, and headed for the door. I put the key on the stand that was behind the couch and left.

SHE DIDN'T HAVE to be happy for me. Nobody did. Long as I

was happy, that was all that mattered. I drove back over to the house. I didn't see Bronte's car. *Of course he wouldn't be here*, I thought. I brought my things in and took them up to the bedroom and started unpacking. It was time to get settled back in.

7

JUNE 02, 2006

L ife with my husband had been simply blissful aside from the demands of running the streets. But when things are going well, you don't go asking for trouble or question certain matters; you just go with it. I finally had gotten the man that I initially fell in love with, back. We got married after the new year at the Justice of the Peace, and I couldn't have been any happier.

Since I was back, I wanted to make things official. We were going into a new year that December I came back, so I wanted to start it off right. Although we got married after two weeks into it, it still was a new beginning. I was officially Golden Wells, and I loved it. I wore my wedding ring proudly.

I shut things down with Will, telling him I was married since he was still texting and calling me. I never really had the time to talk to him. Things were just constantly going on, but he was okay about it. At least that was what he said. I didn't have to worry about doing that with Cortez. I only heard from him from time to time, anyway. I knew he genuinely was concerned about my well-being, so I would answer for him. He always kept things short and sweet.

I never saw Kosha again. Didn't even know how I'd react if I did, but we no longer spoke. I was "living my life like it's Golden" in the words of Jill Scott, because it was. My man was all I needed, and I was finally all he needed.

It was around eight in the evening and Bronte and I were cuddled in the bedroom watching a movie when Bronte was interrupted by a phone call. The second I looked over at him, after a few minutes of talking, he hung up and got out the bed. I noticed him getting dressed.

"Babe, where are you going?"

"I gotta make a run real quick."

I sat up in the bed.

"But you just got in here."

He had only been relaxed, sitting by me for like thirty minutes. The movie had really just started.

"Well, now I needa go back out."

"Bronte, when are you going to stop doing this?"

"When are you gonna stop questioning me about it all the damn time?"

"Until you stop! And to be fair, I haven't said anything about this in a while. You act like you don't be complaining ya damn self. Every time I turn around, you're saying, '*I'm gonna get out the game. I'm tired of the bullshit*', and yet you're still in it."

"I don't see you questioning me about it when you buying shoes, clothes, and new handbags and shit! This damn house," he added. "Get da fuck outta here wit' dat! I ain't tryna hear dat shit right now! I'll be back."

I went back to minding my own business, and about an hour later, I was startled while I was in my bed, by this loud ass banging on my sliding doors.

Boom! Boom! Boom!

"What the fuck! Who is it!" I screamed irate as I swung my body, angrily, as I sat up.

"Baby, it's me! Open the door!"

There was panic and urgency all in his voice. We had a master suite on the first level with sliding doors that led out to the patio. I didn't know why Bronte didn't go to the front door and use his key, but I had to get up.

"Ugh!" I got up and let him in. "You were running from the po-po, weren't you?" He passed out right on the bed, breathing all hard and shit. "Bronte, one of these days you gon' get me caught up in ya shit! I know it!"

He was still trying to catch his breath and talk to me at the same time.

"Look... ain't... no... body... gon' get... caught up in nothing... man. I'm tired. Damn!"

"What happened this time?"

"Hold up... gimme a minute." I stood there, waiting patiently for him to get his lungs out his throat so he could talk. "Alright. All I was doing was meeting up with Wayne. Next thing you know, all these niggas just come sprayin' outta nowhere."

"Niggas? What niggas?"

"Fuck if I know! But we handled who we could... enough to get da fuck outta there."

"Bronte, I better not have the po-po coming to this house looking for you. If they come, I swear I'm turning ya ass in."

"You talking bullshit! It wasn't even no fuckin' cops around, and even if it was, you ain't gon' do nothing but what the fuck you been doing, which is lying."

"No, I'm not! Let 'em come here. Your ass needs to give this shit up!"

He got off the bed and walked out the room. I followed right behind him. He went in the kitchen and opened the refrigerator; I'm sure looking for something to drink and eat since I caught him rubbing his stomach.

"I thought I gave you money to go to the store?"

I leaned on the island.

"I paid a bill with it."

"What bill?"

"My credit card bill."

He looked at the fridge disgusted.

"Whatchu fix to eat then?"

"I ate the rest of the leftovers earlier, and since it

was a little bit of milk left, when I got hungry again, I ate a bowl of cereal."

He slammed the refrigerator door shut and looked in my direction.

"So I guess you expect me to give you some more money for food?"

"I do if you expect me to cook."

"Fuck it! I'll go to the store my damn self." He walked out of the kitchen to leave. I followed him but stopped in the foyer. The minute he opened the door it was a female standing there. "What the fuck is this?"

When I heard Bronte say that, I took a few steps more to see what he was talking about. She was holding a newborn baby in a car seat.

"This is ya son. That's what the fuck this is, and I'm leaving him here with you. Here's all his shit. Birth record in the bag, and his social security card will be coming to this address. Raise ya fuckin' son in ya big ass house!"

"The fuck you mean?" She set that carrier with the baby in it down, along with this big ass duffle bag and diaper bag and jetted off. "Aye, Jackie!"

"Jackie!" I repeated.

The next thing I knew, he went chasing after her, leaving the baby by the door. I couldn't believe this shit. My mind was still stuck on Jackie. Then to see a child sleeping peacefully in front of me that belonged to Bronte, blew my fuckin' mind. None of this seemed real, but seeing this infant that looked like Bronte made it tangible. My heart was crushed. I moved the baby from in front of the door and suddenly heard gunshots.

My feet carried me out of the house so fast, because all that was on my mind was the well-being of Bronte. I didn't care about anything else. I was scared that crazy bitch shot him. I couldn't see any activity, but I instantly started to cry. My emotions crumbled and got the best of me. Then I heard police sirens and ambulances and noticed the direction they were going in, which was opposite of this house.

I ran back inside, grabbed the car seat with the baby in it, and ran around the corner. There was a crowd of people standing around. I pushed my way through but got stopped by one of the officers as I tried to go further than everyone else. The kicker was, at that time, I didn't even notice that officer was Cortez. All I saw was my worst nightmare. Three bodies. Two males, one female. But more importantly, one being Bronte. I tried to get to him and screamed in pure horror the moment I saw him.

"Get the—Get the fuck off me! That's my... ma—!" I could barely breathe, let alone get my words out. It was like my tongue kept getting caught in my throat as I tried to breathe and speak. "My fuckin' husband! Noo wah uh uh uhhh! Brontayeee!" I cried with everything in me, not wanting to believe what I was seeing.

Blood was stained everywhere on the white t-shirt he'd just threw on, as he lie lifeless on the ground. He looked like he had multiple gunshot wounds. My whole world had been changed in an instant. Someone snatched the baby out of my hand as Cortez tried to contain me. I fuckin' lost it as I was being restrained, watching the paramedics put his lifeless looking body in the ambulance.

"Noo wah uh uh uhhh! Brontayeeee... Oh God! Noowaa uhh!"

My knees just buckled underneath me as I bawled my eyes out, and at that point, he released me. I was devastated. Someone else just put their arms around me and held me. I didn't know if he told them to or what, but I felt like I too, was dying. Then I realized I needed to get to the hospital. He was not about to die on me. I flung this stranger's arms off me and jumped up to go to my car.

"Hey! You're forgetting your baby," I heard a voice say. It was a lady holding the child in her arms since he was crying. The woman brought the baby over to me. I just stared at his little face as he screamed at the world from the top of his lungs. "I'm so sorry to hear about your husband, but I think your baby is hungry, sweetheart. I know this is a horrific time for you. Maybe you could get someone to watch him while you go check on your man."

I wasn't even thinking about this child. He wasn't even mine. Then it dawned on me the female that was also shot was his mother, Jackie. I took the baby out of the woman's arms and grabbed the car seat. Then I went inside the house and grabbed his bag and took a bottle out of it.

This child looked only to be at least a month or two, if that. Hell, I didn't know. All I knew was it looked new. Not only did I have to deal with him now, I had to come to grips with Bronte still fucking Jackie and now possibly gone. I put him back in the car seat, strapped him up, and propped the bottle in his mouth before I rushed to the car. They had to have taken them to the nearest hospital *Angelwood General,* which was where I was headed.

Once I arrived, I rushed over to the information desk where two ladies were sitting talking.

"I need information on a gunshot victim, Bronte Wells, that was just brought here."

"You are?" asked a Caucasian woman as she was putting the information in the system.

"I'm his wife. Is he going to be okay?"

"You can head up to the second floor. They can give you more information there."

I sighed from being annoyed. Once she gave me directions on where to go, I flew to the elevators, baby swinging in my hand and all. I checked on him in the elevator, and he was back sleeping, so I tucked the bottle on the side of him. I asked the same thing once I got up to this desk.

"I need information on a gunshot victim, Bronte Wells, that was just brought here."

"Yes, if you would have a seat over there, I'll page his surgeon to come speak to you." She nodded her head at the other lady that was at the desk. That lady ended up leaving.

"All I want to know is if he's alright," I stated, trying to hold it together. "Please just say he's alive. I just want to know that!"

"I understand that, ma'am, which is why we're going to have his surgeon talk to you. I have no answers right now on his condition. Don't worry. He'll be here to speak with you soon." Next, I saw her eyes roll in another direction. "There he is." I turned around and saw a gentleman in a white coat coming toward us. I ended up power walking to him.

"Bronte Wells. Is he gonna be okay? Please, can I see him," I cried as I simultaneously set the car seat down.

The doctor's expression went blank the minute I asked to see him.

"I'm sorry. Unfortunately, the gunshots he sustained were very damaging. They hit major arteries, causing him to lose a lot of blood an—"

"No, don't! Please," I ordered before taking my free hand and covering my mouth, muffling my sobs as they came to the surface. I broke down, not wanting him to confirm what I had already feared.

"I'm so sorry."

I had no more words. My baby was gone. I just cried in my hands.

Shortly after, Cortez came walking up. I didn't even know it until I heard the voice. I opened my eyes.

"Sorry to interrupt, but I need to ask her a few questions once you're done."

"She's all yours, but I would give her a moment."

I gave Cortez the stare of death as I huffed from my grief. I was ready to get in his ass because now was not the time.

"Yes, sir," he responded. The doctor walked back over to the desk. "Before you snap on me, I don't have any questions for you. I'm here because I know what happened to Bronte. I just wanted to be here for you, Gold. Can you walk with me please?"

With my face drenched in tears and nose running, I looked at him, trying to muster up the strength just to leave that spot.

"I can't leave him, Cortez. I need to see him."

"You don't want to see him like that."

My fists were balled at my sides as anger started to fill me.

"Who are you to tell me what I want? I need to see him!"

The next thing I knew, the baby started crying. I knew I hadn't changed his diaper, burped him since he fell asleep, nothing. I couldn't do this. But when I knelt and looked down at his tiny face, all I saw was Bronte. He was all I had left of him.

"Whose baby?"

"... He's mine." I don't know why, but I lied. In a way, he was mine if he was Bronte's son. "I need to go somewhere and change him," I said as I took his bawled-up body out of the seat. Cortez picked it up to carry for me.

"Come with me." I walked with him. He stopped and spoke with one of the ladies at the desk as I was trying to quiet the baby. I still had tears dropping from my own eyes. All of this was so hard to digest. Cortez was on the move again, so I continued to go where he led. It was an empty patient room with a couch in it. I went over to it immediately and changed the baby's diaper. "Wow! You never told me you were pregnant. How come?"

"Didn't tell you I was married either."

"Yeah, I noticed that... the ring."

He ended up sitting on the arm of the couch beside me.

"Uh... Cortez, the other people at the scene that got shot. Did any of them survive?"

"I'm afraid not." Since the baby was still crying, I gave him the rest of his bottle. I knew it was cold, but I didn't know what else to do about warming it, and he was fussing. "You should really get him home. There's nothing else you can do here."

"I'm not leaving until I see my husband," I snapped.

"I saw him, Golden. It's not a pretty sight. You don't want that to be your last image of him. Do you?"

"I don't care!" My tone lowered as I thought about him running out of the house being my last time seeing him alive. It choked me up even more knowing I would never see him again. "He's my... my husband dammit," I solemnly muttered. I took the bottle out of the baby's mouth and adjusted myself to look at Cortez. "Do you know what happened?"

"It's still being investigated, but it looked like an intended shooting. That's all I can say."

My eyes beamed on him like a spotlight.

"Well, shouldn't you be helping with that instead of sitting here with me?"

"What I should be doing and what I want to be doing don't always go hand in hand."

By now, I was trying to burp the baby and not having much success. I was so emotional. Just thinking about who wanted to kill Bronte and why was so disturbing.

"Why you always say that shit to me! I'm serious, Cortez! I need answers!"

"We're going to get to the bottom of it. My partner and I are interviewing witnesses as we speak." I gave him another death stare. "I had to see how you were, Gold. You were in pretty bad shape at the crime scene. I knew you would come here, and I'd catch you... I just wanted to help in any way I could. Now, I need your help too. I really need you to take that baby and yourself home."

"What are you doing here in *Arcchester* anyway?"

Again, I was shocked and annoyed at bumping into him it seemed, at my lowest moments.

"I live here. I never knew you were here."

"I wasn't at first. We moved here after the new year. Oh my God!" I cried as a rush of feelings let panic set in. "I can't believe this is really happening."

"Okay, that's it. You need to get out of here."

I spoke to him through gritted teeth.

"How many times do I have to tell you that I'm not

leaving here until I see Bronte? Now since you didn't let me find out from the doctor if I could see him, you will be escorting me to see my husband!"

He put his hands up and gave in.

"I'll see what I can do. Is there anyone you'd like for me to contact?"

I sniffled before answering.

"I can't really answer that. I've never met his family. All I know is his mother lives in *Onibury,* and I only know that much because I heard one of his boys asking about her, and that's what he told him. Bronte never shared much about his family. Neither did I."

"Okay. Not a problem. That's not too far away."

Since the baby was finally asleep, I bundled him back up and put him back in his car seat. We ended up going to the morgue in the hospital. Cortez did all the talking to the gentleman that was there as I prepared myself as much as I could for what I was about to see. He stayed on the outside with the baby so I could go in.

I was foolish to think you could prepare for such a thing. I could have never been prepared to see my husband in this state. I ran out of there and threw up in the hallway, damn near choking as I cried in between hurling. Down on my hands and knees, I felt like the wind had been knocked out of me, and there was no air to revive me.

Cortez swept me in his loving arms, pulling me away from my puddle and held me up, as my limp body could barely stand. He kissed my temple as he sympathized with my pain. The man in the morgue came and gave Cortez some tissue for me and noticed the vomit. Eventually, I collected myself and was ready to get out of there.

Cortez walked me out of the hospital carrying the baby seat. As we were on our way through the revolving doors, Kosha just so happened to be coming in and spotted me. She waited until I came through to the outside and grabbed me, wrapping her arms around my neck.

"Oh my God, bitch!" She was crying. "I'm so happy to see you! I thought you were dead."

I yanked her arms off me.

"Get the fuck out my face."

"What?" she squealed, puzzled by my reaction.

I started walking. Cortez was still standing there with her. He yelled my name.

"Golden!"

"I'm leaving!"

She came running beside me.

"I'm sorry! Golden, let's put this bullshit behind us, okay! I wanna be there for you. I know how much you loved him."

Filled with aggravation, I stopped walking and spoke to her.

"Bitch, you threatened to tell my husband about Will, when it wasn't shit to tell. You hated Bronte, and now you want things to be all good because my husband is dead? Bitch, bye!"

I turned away from her and walked faster to my car.

"I would've never told him!" she yelled. "Fuck! I said that in anger."

Cortez made it up to the car since I was already in it. He strapped the baby in the back seat. He didn't say shit about the situation. He made sure I was secure.

"You sure you're okay to drive?"

I figured he was referring to the puffiness of my wet eyes and my current state of mind considering how emotional I was.

"I'll be fine."

"I'm going to call you tonight. Make sure you answer the phone."

"I'm not in the mood for talking anymore, Cortez."

"I'll just be checking on you. That's all."

"Fine. I'll answer."

"Drive safe."

I started up the car and left. Once I got in the house, I grabbed the baby's things and took them with me to the bedroom. In that moment, I realized I had nothing. Who was I kidding? There was no way I could keep this baby. I had nothing else to give anymore. How could I give anything to this very dependent child?

My mind was racing as I undressed him and laid him in our bed. If it wasn't for this little life, and me seeing Bronte's corpse with my own eyes, I'd have sworn none of this was real. The tears were on the brink as I sat on the bed and was slowly coming to terms that all of this was very real and left on me.

It broke my heart as I looked around the room, tearful, that Bronte would never come in here again. He would never hold me and make love to me. This shit fuckin' hurt! I couldn't hold it in and released more cries. I ran in the bathroom not to wake up the baby and sat on the toilet and wept inside of my shirt. I was so tired of losing the people that I loved. It never seemed to end. I didn't know what my life was going to look like now without Bronte in it. It was unimaginable.

All of a sudden, I heard my phone. I didn't even know where it was. I got up listening for the direction of the sound. When I came out of the bathroom, I saw it was in the car seat. I had so many missed calls. I didn't even realize my phone had been going off. It started to chime again. It was Cortez. I wiped my eyes and sniffled and cleared my throat before answering so he'd think I had gotten it together.

"Hello."

"Just calling to check on you."

It didn't work. The moment I heard his voice, I continued to cry.

"I'm not doing so good. This shit hurts so bad," I whined.

"I'm sorry you're hurting, love. I really am. Damn, man... There's no one that can be with you for a few nights?"

"No-oh." I sniffled once more and wiped my eyes.

"Don't take this the wrong way but why don't you and the

baby come and stay with me for a while. Maybe you shouldn't be there just yet, especially alone."

"Auh, auhn... no... I can't, Cortez."

"I just hate that you're there alone."

"I need to be here!" I quieted down. "Don't worry about me. I'm used to being alone."

He sighed.

"You don't have to be alone, Golden. Let someone be there for *you*, for a change."

"I gotta go. Thanks for checking on me. I'll be fine. Good night, Cortez."

After speaking with him, I wasn't in the mood to talk to no one else. I was surprised I saw calls from Will and Kosha. I wondered if my not answering was what made her go to the hospital. Damn, news traveled fast, and I wasn't in the mood to tell people what the fuck I didn't even know myself. I got in the shower and cried some more. Then I got in the bed and slept until I heard a baby crying, waking me up. This was not my life.

8

JUNE 26, 2006

Bronte's funeral had been arranged by his boys and held on June 12, 2006. I was in no shape to plan anything. When that day came, it was a disaster. I saw that bald-headed bitch that came to his house the day he proposed and lost it. Right when we were exiting the church and headed to go to the burial, I saw her. I left the baby in the pew and ran over to the row she was in since she was still sitting there. I saw her look up as she noticed me.

"What the fuck you doing here?"

She looked around at everyone that was starting to stare at us.

"I'm here to pay my respects."

"You don't belong here. Get out!" I ordered.

Two of Bronte's boys, Jyreese and Wiz, were near and came over. Wiz put his hands on my shoulders.

"Gold, come on."

"Get the fuck off me, Wiz," I fussed as I still had my eyes on this bitch. I never even knew her name, but I'd never forget her ugly ass face.

"I loved him too, whether you want to hear that or not."

We stared each other in the eyes for a few seconds after she said that. A surge of anger just took over me, and I back handed her. Wiz pulled my arms behind me like the police. That bitch was holding her face stunned. Everyone else was stunned too.

"I better not see yo' ass at the burial! I swear you'll be in that dirt so fast!"

Embarrassed by the many stares, that bitch left out of the church. Jyreese had nothing to say as he stared at me the whole time. Next thing I knew, I was being approached by Bronte's mother. I had never spoken to her or ever been formally intro-duced. This was our first meeting, and she didn't look happy to see me at all. Her eyes were red, and her expression was filled with fury.

"Are you crazy! This is how you honor my son? This is the type of behavior you embrace at his funeral?"

I stood my ground.

"She had no right to be here."

His mother got in my face.

"If you think she's the only one sitting in this church that my son messed with, you are dumber than you just looked fighting."

"Excuse me?"

"I'm not even sure if you should be taking care of that baby acting like this! Who just leaves a baby!"

At this point, since she obviously had no respect for me, the gloves were off.

"The baby's mother, but if you can do so much better, Ms. Wells, you take him. Be my guest!"

"Maybe I will! You're a disgrace as his wife. I see why we never met."

"We never met because you weren't important enough for him to introduce me to. Just like you weren't important enough to come to our wedding."

His mother let out a faint laugh.

"You call that a wedding? Humph! I know one thing I'm coming to. To legally get my grandson."

She raised her eyebrows at me before she started walking away.

"Good! Don't take too long!"

No words could describe my pain that day, but I knew we all were grieving, and maybe I shouldn't have behaved in that manor, but I was hurting and didn't need stupid bitches there to add to it. That one bitch wasn't at his burial, that was for sure, and if it was others there, like his mother said, well, I had no clue who they were. If she wanted to come and take BJ, she was more than welcome to. I ain't have time for none of this shit. Sad thing too, I never expected our encounter to be like that, but hey, the moment you show me disrespect, none will be given back.

We did get married without her knowledge, so that could be a part of her distaste for me too. I didn't know. The whole situation was tragic, and the bottom line was, this child didn't have either one of his parents and since I'd had him, I had been questioning if I was fit to take on that task myself. Oh, I did look at his birth record that was in that bag, and his name was also, Bronte. Bronte O'rien Wells Jr. He was born May 2, 2006.

His son was the splitting image of him. I couldn't even find fault with that. He legit stole his face, and looking at it reminded me daily of what I didn't have. These past few weeks with everything that had happened, I couldn't sleep, had barely been eating, and was not in the mood for company and conversation of any kind. I just wanted to be left alone.

Cortez had to come by today though. He had some questions for me. *Police business*, he said. He had only given me a few days after the funeral before he said he had to come by. I prolonged it even more, until now. The thought of him further tormenting my brain with questions was discouraging me. I was feeding the baby when he arrived.

"Hey!" His eyes roamed around the house. Fortunately, for me, cleaning was what I did best and mostly what I'd done, when BJ allowed, to take my mind off things. "Nice place you got here."

"Thank you." He followed me into the sitting room. I had a seat. Like the gentleman Cortez was, he stood. "Don't know how much longer I'll be in here though, but that's not what you came for. Let's get this over with."

"Well, I'll get straight to the point. We've been trying to look into the whereabouts of Jackie's baby. We know she recently had an infant, which Bronte is allegedly the father of. It was brought to our attention that she was bringing the baby here. We're just following up, making sure, if necessary, the child is placed in the proper care. Would you happen to know anything about this?"

This had Bronte's mother written all over it to me. I knew I lied and told Cortez he was my son, but I knew I needed to tell him the truth. I propped BJ on my shoulder to burp him as I came clean.

"Cortez, this is the baby that Jackie had."

He didn't seem surprised.

"I had a feeling, but I had hoped you didn't lie to me."

"Technically, it's not a lie. I'm Bronte's wife, which makes BJ my stepson."

"Since the mother is also deceased, we need to do a DNA test on the baby to make sure Bronte is the father."

"I can look at this baby and know he's Bronte's."

"And if that's the case then legally you would be his guardian, but if not, then..."

"You'll take him," I concluded.

"You don't seem upset by that."

My eyes veered away from Cortez. He was right. I wasn't upset. These past weeks had shown me that I just might not be the best option for him. Plus, I knew if Bronte's mother was behind this, then the baby could just live with her.

"What if the DNA test confirms that the child is Bronte's? Would I still have to care for him?"

"May I?" That made Cortez want to take a seat beside me. "Why wouldn't you want to continue to care for your deceased husbands' child?"

I got up and placed the baby in the car seat and continued to look at BJ as I sat back down.

"I can't care for him. I don't know what I'm doing half the time, myself. This responsibility, I thought... I thought I could handle because it was the right thing to do but..." I turned to Cortez. "I can't. I have nothing to give to him. He has no furniture, soon I'll be running out of formula and pampers... I can't even get him to stop crying half the time when he's not sleeping..."

He put his hand over mine.

"Hey! Hey! It's going to be alright. Let's just take this one step at a time, okay. We'll get the DNA test done first and then take it from there. In the meantime, you know I'm here. You need anything, call me. No matter the time." His coffee brown eyes glistened as he seriously gazed at me. "You hear me?"

"Yes."

I moved my hand from under him and latched it on to my arm as I rubbed it.

"You wouldn't have heard about the baby from Bronte's mother, would you?"

I gazed at him, hopeful.

"You know I can't give you any information like that...
She did speak to my partner."

"Hm. I'm sure."

"One more question. Do you know what Bronte was
doing before the shooting? Was he at home...? Did he say
where he was going before it happened...?"

"Uh..." It took me a moment to get my head around that
night again. "Right before that, he came racing in the house...
Someone was chasing him and his boy Wayne, he said. He
didn't know why. Then shortly after that, Jackie showed up at
our door with the baby. She just dropped him off inside our
door and left. Bronte went chasing after her, and that's
when..." I took a deep breath from the anguish of reliving it
all. "That's all I know. I was here with the baby."

"So, did you already know about the baby... or you didn't
know..."

I was embarrassed to admit anything, but I answered
him.

"No. I uh... I knew nothing."

"I'm sorry." He stood up. "Well, I better get going. I'll be in
touch as far as the DNA test. Until then, don't hesitate to call
me." I walked Cortez to the door. "For what's it's worth, that
baby needs you, especially if he turns out to be Bronte's, and
you may just find a part of you needs him too."

With that being said, he left. I went and cuddled up
back on the couch while BJ slept. I finally decided to listen
to my messages. I had so many missed calls, and my

mailbox was full. I had messages from a few of Bronte's boys, Will, and Kosha. I called Bronte's boy Jyreese. He said it was urgent, and when we talked, he wanted to come by, so I told him he could and waited for him to arrive. Finally, he was here.

"How you doing, baby girl?" I eyed him like he was fuckin' crazy for asking. "I know. I know. Don't worry doe. We gon' take care of things."

"What you mean?"

He started staring at the baby. His face grew sour.

"Damn! His soldier gon' be alright, fo'sho."

Now I was getting irritated.

"Reese, what's up?"

He faced me.

"Oh! I got some baby stuff out in the truck. I been tryna drop it off, but you were in a bad space, so I was just waiting for you to call me."

"What stuff?"

"I'm about to bring it in. Also, no need to worry about the bills and shit. We got you. My mans might not be here to take care of things anymore, but his boys got his back, always." My hands covered my nose and mouth, shocked. "Lemme go bring this stuff in. I'll be right back."

He came in with a beautiful portable crib bed that was put together. Went back out and brought in a regular crib that was in a box and then came back in again with a bunch of big shopping bags that I had to go through to see what was in them. His lean body worked up a sweat. I went to get him a water bottle. Still stunned, I handed him the water.

"Ho-how did you know I needed anything."

"Well, I knew you didn't have the baby until the shooting, and then the way you and his moms was going at it, I didn't wanna give her no more ammunition to use against you if she tried to take my mans."

"So you don't think he should go with her?"

"Hell no! Bronte wouldn't want dat shit either. Only thing she would be concerned wit' would be dat check every month. She barely cared about her own damn son, which is why he got her the fuck away from him the second he could. Moved her ass right out of here."

"I never knew that. He never spoke to me about his family."

"Yeah, he didn't speak to anybody about 'em, really. I've just been around him to see shit."

"Hm." That had me curious. "Reese, did Bronte know about the baby?"

He was busy guzzling down that water. Then he let out a huge burp.

"Damn! My bad!" Nah but... c'mon, baby girl. You know I wouldn't tell you even if I did know. Bottom-line. You were always wifey... before the ring. My nigga loved you. That's real." None of that made me feel any better, and I honestly believed Bronte didn't know, but that was neither here nor there at this point. "I'm out! You got the number. Let me know when the bills start coming in, and I'll send you money." He started walking to the door. "Take care of little mans. If you find you need other stuff, let me know."

I shut that door, still in shock about the info on his mother, along with having all this baby stuff. The first thing I did was wiped the portable crib down and then laid BJ in it. Then I sat on the couch and went through what was in the bags. He had everything under the sun in them. Part of me was grateful to have it since he didn't have anything, but I still didn't know how I felt about raising him and messing up his life like mine. I may not have put his life in Bronte's mother's hands, but that didn't mean it had to stay in mine.

As I was pulling items out, my cell phone started going off again. I saw it was Will. I decided to go ahead and answer, since he along with everyone else had been trying to get in touch with me since the shooting. I put the call on speaker so my hands could still be free.

"Hello!"

"Yo, Gold! Man! I've been trying for days to reach you. Yo! You don't know how good it feels to finally hear you, man."

"I know. My phone has been ringing nonstop. I just wasn't ready to talk to anyone."

"I'm sorry for your loss, ma. Fo' real."

"Thanks, Will."

"How you been making out?"

"As good as can be expected."

While I was viewing one of BJ's outfits in my hand, he

started crying. I swear at times I felt like I didn't know what to do for him when he was awake. I would feed him and change him, and he'd still cry.

"You got company?"

"No," I said as I was headed to the portable crib. I picked up BJ and walked back by the phone.

"You babysitting?"

"No, Will. I'm not. It's my son, and I need to change him, so I gotta go."

"Ya son? When did you have a baby? I never even knew you were pregnant."

"Look, that doesn't matter. I'll have to talk to you later."

"Okay, but before you go, can I at least come see you? I got something for you."

"What could you possibly have for me?" I asked as I tried to talk over BJ's crying.

"It's just a little something I got after I heard about what happened. I can meet you or do whatever you feel. I'm gonna be in town for a while so... I just wanna give you what I have."

"I'll text you my address. I gotta go though."

"Okay! Don't forget to text it to me."

I hung up. I didn't think BJ could be hungry so soon, so I just changed him. Then I spotted a new pacifier, which I'd never had before. I ended up giving it to him. He quieted down and actually went back to sleep. I laid him back down and went back to going through his things. I did return a few more calls to Bronte's boys that called me. Cortez called while I was on the phone with one of them. He gave the information on getting an appointment to get the DNA test done on BJ. *That was fast*, I thought. Now I just needed to call and set up an appointment.

9

JULY 05, 2006

I was able to bring BJ in to get testing done fairly quickly since it was a part of an investigation. Cortez went with me. The procedure didn't take long at all. We were in and out. I waited until we were in the hallway before I spoke to him about Bronte.

"Have you had any leads on who killed Bronte?"

"We're close."

That took me by surprise. We continued to walk out the building together.

"Really?"

"Yeah. He's not the trigger finger, but if we can get him to talk it would make things a lot easier. But once I have something more concrete to tell you, I will."

I sighed with a bit of relief. I just wanted whoever that did that to my baby to pay. But knowing Bronte's boys, justice was going to be served either way.

"So what happens now with BJ?"

"You'll continue to care for the baby. They'll enforce a subpoena to have the body exhumed and do the testing. Once we have the results, we'll let you know. What's wrong?"

My face, I'm sure, showed my apprehension for all of this, which likely caused him to be concerned. While we continued to walk to my car, I answered his question.

"Cortez, none of this has been easy for me. I cry all the time. He cries all the time. I really don't think I should keep him."

We got to my car, and Cortez fastened the baby in before he responded.

"I'm sure you're just being hard on yourself." He opened my door for me. "I'll be off for a few days. I'll come help you. How 'bout that?"

"Can you help for eighteen years?" I asked, staring him down.

"I could, if you let me, but I know you don't mean that."

I rolled my eyes at him and sucked my teeth.

"You get my point. You helping me for a few days doesn't solve my issue."

I finally sat down in the seat. He closed the door and waited for me to roll the window down. A headache was on the verge. I knew I hadn't eaten, but I wasn't hungry. I think the news of them being close to finding Bronte's killer brought on tension.

"I think you feel this way regarding the baby because you're still grieving, and you haven't had any peace of mind to do that. A lot has changed for you overnight. You really shouldn't be alone."

"So you've said," I reminded him.

"What about that girl that was at the hospital? Since you won't let me be there for you, what about her?"

"Fuck her!"

"Come on now, Gold. If it's one thing I know about life, it can be messy, and people make mistakes. I don't know what your issue is with her, but she seemed to want to make things right, in light of realizing life's too short to hold grudges. My assumption, of course."

"She's been calling, but I don't know. I really don't think I can forgive her."

"Is what she did that unforgivable?"

"I don't really want to think about her right now. My head is already starting to hurt. Anyway, I better get home before the scream machine wakes up while I'm driving."

"Aw, give 'em a break. He's adjusting too."

"Whatever."

"I'll be in touch."

Since I was expecting Will, I drove home. Part of me was thinking about calling him and telling him this wasn't a good idea. My head was throbbing a bit more, and I knew I was about to be even more of a bitch. Why he had something for me, I had no clue. I didn't even know why I agreed to let him bring it to me, but the way I was feeling, this visit was going to be short lived.

I got out of the car, grabbed the baby, and began to open the door. I set the car seat down once inside, and that was all I remembered. When I opened my eyes, Will was sitting beside me on the couch holding the baby.

"Here, you need to drink this." I was still trying to figure out what was going on. I felt a cold compress on my head, at the same time as him stuffing a water bottle down my throat with his free hand. Multitasking at its best. My face automatically distorted, confused.

"Mm... Will, wha—"

"Shhh... drink first." I quieted and drank the water. I didn't realize how thirsty I was and drank it all. Then I shifted myself upward even more. "Easy now."

"What happened?" I asked, still groggy.

"I came up to the door thinking you left it open because I was coming here and saw you laid out on the floor by the car seat. I didn't realize it was a baby still in there until I got you on the couch and lil' dude started fussing."

"Oh my gosh." I panicked as I tried to grab him from Will, but he stopped me.

"The baby, as you can see, is fine. My concern right now is you. Are you in pain anywhere?"

"No. I had a slight headache, but that was all. I don't

know why that happened."

"You ain't been taking care of yourself, have you?"

"I'm fine."

"You're not fine! Did you not hear me say you were passed out when I got here? What if I wasn't coming through?" He didn't even give me a chance to answer. "What you have for breakfast? What you eat period today? Lately! Because I know you, and when shit go sour you shut down."

I raised my voice as I pointed in his face.

"Nigga, you don't have the right to act like you care! So don't fuckin' question me like I'm ya damn child."

I learned fast it was a bad idea to yell. I laid back.

"I do care, Gold, and stop yelling in front of ya baby like that."

What was really tripping me out too, was as this mother-fucka held BJ, he was laying there just as quiet, looking at who knows what. That shit got under my skin.

"Oh, what *do you* know," I sassed, waving him off.

He started shaking his head back and forth.

"You're not going to pick an argument so you can get me to leave. I'mma do you a favor." He stared at BJ briefly. "I'mma take one for the team and change... yo... what's lil' dude's name?"

"BJ."

"Alright, well, I'mma change him and give him a bottle for you. Then I'mma fix you something to eat."

"You don't have to do this. I *am* capable."

"I know what you're capable of, but apparently you ain't been doing what you're capable of, so I will, at least for today. Besides, I want to. I got time. I'm here so... deal with it."

Watching him change BJ only confirmed what I knew about him. He would've been a great father. I mean, he wasn't perfect at changing him, from how awkward he looked, but he didn't look like a fish out of water either. That made me also think about something I had been avoiding. Bronte, how he would've been with BJ. I thought all the time about how surprised he was when Jackie came here.

Since then, I had been convincing myself that once I finally moved in, that he had changed. That Jackie had already been pregnant, and he didn't know. It's plausible, since he really seemed surprised by her arrival and the baby. But then again, I thought maybe it was just that. The fact that she had the balls to bring him to Bronte with the expectation of him raising his son by himself. Maybe he did know about him. Unfortunately, that's something I'd never know, and it constantly ate me alive. Will had said something, bringing me out of my thoughts, then I realized he was talking to the baby as he was feeding him. Then we got to talking.

"So you said you had something for me. What is it?" I asked.

"Oh!" he said like he just remembered it. "I think my gift is perfect too." He leaned over a tad since his hands were full feeding the baby. "Reach in my back pocket."

When I dug in them, he had a folded envelope in it. I

held it, flipping it over on each side as I eyed it.

"This?"

"Yeah! Open it."

When I opened it, it was a gift card to be pampered at *la Salle da Rose.* I didn't know how to react. First of all, this place was too high class for my ass and extremely expensive.

"Why would you get me this?"

"I figured with everything you're going through, maybe this could help you relieve some stress, even for a moment, and to also just give you a chance to relax."

Will changed positions once he took BJ's bottle out his mouth and had him on his shoulder. He was fast asleep, likely not going to burp.

"I appreciate the gesture, but there's no way I could accept this. I don't even know when I'd be able to use it, especially since I have BJ."

"Lemme know when you tryna go, and I'll watch the baby."

I busted out laughing. The first in weeks. BJ rolled his eyes that were still half asleep after my outburst, like I disturbed him. His little mouth hung open afterwards as he breathed like he was exhausted.

"What you know about watching a child?"

"I bet I know more than you. I have my cousin's kids occasionally and have had experiences with them as babies since I've matured," he bragged.

"I can't argue with you there. I've had none." I shook my

head, as BJ had my attention. "Look at him. I haven't heard him whoop and holler at all since you've had him. It's like the minute he sees me, he turns into a scream machine and cries, making it harder for me to comfort him."

"Babies can sense things. Maybe he can feel that you're tense and stressed." I kept shaking my head back and forth, not knowing what to think. I knew I wasn't his mother, nor did I want to be, but I was really trying. He went and laid the baby down. "So what you wanna eat?"

"I don't know. I really don't have a taste for anything."

"I'll find something. You're eating," he ordered before walking to the kitchen.

I got up and went to the bathroom. That made me think about my period. I hadn't gotten it yet. As I sat on the toilet, I got to thinking about when I had it last.

"Shit! No, God, no," I whined as I looked to the ceiling. "Please just let it be late. Please!" I wiped myself and got up. Then while I was washing my hands, it made me realize if I were pregnant, I would have my own child with Bronte. I tried to see it as a good thing, but what wasn't, was raising two kids alone once it was proven that BJ is Bronte's. I shook the thought off. "Give it a few more days, Gold, then go buy a test."

I couldn't remember when I was on last anyway to say I was late, but I did know I had sex with Bronte the night before he was killed, which worried me. I tried to calm down. I took a deep breath before walking out the bathroom. Once

I came back and got comfortable again, I noticed I had a missed call from Cortez. I called him back immediately, hoping he had some news about Bronte.

"Hey! You called me?"

"Hey! How you feeling?"

"I'm fine. Any news?"

I heard him smiling through the phone.

"Didn't I tell you I would let you know that?"

"I thought that was why you were calling."

"No. I was just checking on you since your head had been bothering you. And so you know, I would come and tell you news like that in person. Not over the phone."

"Oh."

I felt disappointed.

"You okay?"

"Gold, you got any garlic powder?" I looked over in the direction of the kitchen since we had an open concept. "Oh, never mind."

"You got company?"

"Yeah."

"You mind my asking who?"

"He's just a friend, Cortez. Stop tryna play detective."

"No one's doing that."

I rolled my eyes.

"Yeah, okay."

"The baby sleep?"

"Yeah, thank God!"

"Well, like I said earlier, I'll be off for a few days, so if it's okay with you, I can come by there... help you out if it's some things you wanted to do that BJ is keeping you from."

"Yeah! Sleep!"

Since Cortez was several years older than his sister Giselle and myself, I knew he had experience just from being a big brother. For some reason, I didn't have any doubts that he could handle BJ, and honestly, BJ was tiring me out. At least I hoped it was from him.

"You got it! I'll be over first thing."

"I'm sure I'll be up."

"Well, I'll let you get back to your company. If you need me to bring you anything for tomorrow, call me."

"I'll keep that in mind."

From smelling the food cooking, it was making me hungry. In the next few minutes, Will was bringing me a plate. He made me a cheeseburger with French fries. Then, after he brought me that, he came back with a glass of red wine. He sat it down on the table.

"What? Why you looking at the glass like that? Too much?"

I really didn't know if I should have drunk it or not.

"Oh n-nothing. It's perfect." The minute I was about to take a bite of my burger, BJ started crying. "Oh my gosh!" I complained.

"You go 'head and eat. I'll get him. Chill," he said, sounding positive.

"He has a pacifier somewhere around here. He shouldn't be hungry already."

"Nah, I got 'em."

Now I was chewing with animosity. He was so good with him, I hated it. I didn't understand why the fuck that child wouldn't take to me, especially since I was the one taking care of him, possibly temporarily at this rate. I couldn't deal with this shit, and if I found out that I was pregnant, ain't no way in hell I was raising two babies on my own.

"Oh, I have a basket sitting in the foyer for little man with some things in it. I had got something for him too, once you told me you had a son," he said as he was rocking BJ back to sleep.

"This food is good, Will."

"You hear what I said?"

"I heard you."

"I noticed you have a whole lot of shit for him already."

"Yeah, but that's because he didn't have anything. I wasn't prepared for him."

He laid him back down.

"I'mma go get it so you can see it."

"You can just put it over there with the rest of his things. Thank you," I said casually. He did just that. "Are you going to eat?"

"I did a little tasting as I fixed it. I'mma clean up the kitchen and then head out. Let you rest while he's sleeping. At least that's what you need to be doing."

"Okay."

He cleaned up as intended and left. I had a rough night with BJ afterwards. I didn't even go back in my bedroom. Once Will left, it was around nine at night. I laid there on the couch. BJ started crying around midnight. I picked him up and put his pacifier in his mouth while I went to warm him some milk. His tiny mouth spit that pacifier out and had a fit. One thing for certain, was this baby had some lungs on him. He was a handful with a big voice.

"Okay, BJ, I'm making you something now, baby." I soothed him as I cradled him in my arms. Once I put the bottle in his mouth, he sucked on the nipple for a few pulls and then began screaming like the scream machine he was. I put him on my shoulder, hoping the position change would calm him. Got more of the same. "BJ, what do you want from me!" I was at my wit's end with him. Frustration set in long ago, and I just didn't want to deal with this much longer. By now, I was in tears too. I rocked him once more. Since he continued to cry, I decided to check his diaper. He was wet, but that still didn't stop him from fussing after he was changed. I covered my face with my hands as he continued to lay there on his back wailing, since I hadn't picked him back up yet. I felt like I was ready to pull my fuckin' hair out. "Jesus, BJ! I don't know what's wrong! What do you want?" I screamed as if he could tell me. I didn't know what to do to stop him from crying, so I called Will. I anxiously awaited as it rang. "Please ,Will, pick up."

He answered half sleep.

"Gold, what's wrong?"

I was bawling right along with BJ.

"I ca-can't get him to stop crying."

"It's gon' be okay. Stop crying. Did you feed him or check his diaper?"

"I did both. He... He won't stop crying, Will. I don't know what else to do. He hates me."

"Pick him up and put him on your shoulders and rub his back till I get there. I'm on my way."

It took Will about twenty minutes to get here. When he arrived, BJ was back to sleep. He had a hefty load that he had let loose in his pamper, and once that was out of his belly he went to sleep. Will watched him sleeping peacefully in his bed.

"What happened? How'd you get him to sleep?"

"I guess rubbing his back helped. He pooped, and once he did that, he quieted down and went to sleep."

"He had gas. You ever think that maybe the milk he's drinking might need to be changed?"

I cut my eyes at him for even asking me that, knowing I seemingly didn't have a maternal instinct in my body. I walked back over and got on the couch.

"No! That never crossed my mind."

"Won't you go get in your bed, and I'll handle little man for the night."

I was so tired, and him saying that was like I had struck

gold, which was uninterrupted sleep.

"Are you sure, Will?"

"Yeah! I'll sleep out here on the couch."

"There are bedrooms upstairs, you know, if you want to carry him upstairs with you."

"This cool! Just give me some blankets, and you can go to bed." I couldn't stop staring at Will and thinking about his generosity. I really didn't know him anymore. "I say something wrong?"

"No. I'll be right back with that blanket."

I dashed to the closet and grabbed him some covers so I could try to get a good night's rest. Lord knows I needed it.

THE NEXT MORNING, I woke up from my phone ringing. It was Cortez. I was yawning as I answered it, still trying to wake up.

"Hello."

"Hey! Good morning!"

I was still tryna open my eyes.

"Good morning," I said, all rusty.

"I'mma stop and pick us up some breakfast. What you want?"

"Anything is fine." I yawned again. "I'm sleepy."

"The baby had you up again, huh?"

"No."

"Well, I'll be there shortly."

"Okay."

I hung up and went back to sleep. When I woke up again, I heard voices. I forgot that fast that Cortez was on his way. I also forgot Will was here. I dragged myself up and went to freshen up in the bathroom first. Then with my robe on, I went out to find the men. They were out in the living room. I smelled food too.

"Good morning," they both said when they saw me enter the room.

"I was fixing you some breakfast," said Will.

"I brought you some breakfast, as discussed," Cortez reminded as his eyes directed me to the food in his hands.

My eyes strolled back and forth at the both of them.

"Thank you both. Will, Cortez. Cortez, Will," I introduced. "In case you two were wondering."

Both their faces showed they really didn't care who the other was. I noticed BJ was sound asleep in his portable crib.

"I'mma go continue making this food. No need in it going to waste since it's already been prepped."

Will headed to the kitchen.

"I'm sorry, Cortez. I forgot he was here."

He stared at me with one eyebrow raised. Next thing I knew, he was in detective mode. This went on for a good minute before he chilled with some of his concern.

"So, Will... He's the guy's name you mentioned when you were arguing with your friend."

"You don't miss anything."

"Who is he?"

"He's my ex-boyfriend."

That made Cortez set the food down on the coffee table. He folded his muscular arms in front of him as his facial expression turned more curious.

"He's here why exactly?"

I plopped down on the couch. When I did that, Will entered back in the room.

"You ready to eat?"

"I don't think she made it clear to you what she wanted to eat," Cortez interjected.

I stood up and got in between them. Even though they weren't standing near each other I wanted to keep it that way.

"Will, thank you for everything. Cortez is going to be helping me out today, so thanks again for all your help with BJ."

"Alright. Well if you need me again like you did last night, *call me*," he emphasized.

That put a smirk on Cortez's face. Will came over to me and gave me a hug. I definitely wasn't expecting that, but I went along with it and hugged him back. Then he left. I clasped my hands together.

"So! What'd you get us to eat?"

"I wasn't sure if you wanted what he had or what I have."

"Well, you did buy me breakfast, and it would be rude of me to allow you to waste your money."

"You know what, whatever you want to pick is fine."

Cortez had stopped at *The Vanilla Brewery*. They had really good food. He began taking it out of the bags. "They have amazing chicken and waffles, so I thought I'd get you that."

"Aw, you remembered."

I took a seat.

"You'd be surprised to know all the things I remembered." I knew he meant that. He and I had a lot of memories over food, but now wasn't the time to be reminiscing. I noticed he also had two bottles of orange juice. He went and warmed my food for me and then placed it in front of me. Before I could even dig in, BJ was awakening. I heard his little engine starting to rev up, which instantly made me tear my face up while I whined.

"Really, BJ!"

"You go 'head and eat. I'mma go wash my hands again, and I'll get him for you."

Cortez hadn't even started eating yet, and I knew he was hungry too. He was a hefty size, all muscle, and could put some food away. But as an officer, he had to stay in shape, and that, he was. He came a long way from when I stayed at his parents' house with his sister, that's for damn sure. He made his way over to BJ, picked him up, and started talking to him first. BJ wasn't tryna hear shit. He was getting his cry on as per usual.

"Okay, lil' man," he said, rocking him as he cradled him. "I got you. You want some food, huh? Yeah, I feel you. I do too, but you more important right now." He walked to the fridge with him and grabbed a bottle, popped it in the microwave for a few, and when he walked back in the living room, I saw him testing it on the back of his hand. "Perfect!"

I sat there and ate my food, watching him as he fed him. It made me think about what Will said about him possibly needing his formula changed, because he damn sure did turn into a scream machine after that milk settled on his tummy at times. I was going to pay attention to that today.

"He needs a bath too."

Cortez raised his head to look over at me.

"Oh, you're really going to put me to work today, aren't you?"

I looked at him and smiled.

"I mean, you volunteered to be here sowa..."

"Nah, it's all good. So what happened last night to make you call ya ex over? Don't think I didn't notice how you never said."

"You don't miss shit! How dare me not notice that."

"You know you could've called me."

I finished chewing the waffle I had in my mouth.

"It wasn't like that. He had already been over and handled BJ with no problems. The minute he left, and BJ woke up, I couldn't get him to stop crying. I didn't know what else to do, so that's when I called Will."

"So what'd he do that was so special to get him to stop crying?"

I started laughing, and lately they were hard to come by. I

stared at him sideways.

"Are you jealous of my relationship with Will?" I toyed. "'Cause you've really been grilling me today."

He answered unbothered.

"Yeah right."

"He didn't do anything but tell me to rub his back till he got here. I don't know if he knew that would help or not. Once I did that, BJ had an explosion in his pamper, and then he went to sleep."

"So he had gas."

I shook my head, feeling like a dumb ass for not figuring that out. Cortez was shifting the baby so he could burp him.

"Yeah! But Will seems to think since he cries like that a lot, maybe I should see about getting his formula changed. I said I was going to keep an eye out on his behavior today."

"Oh, so maybe he does know a little something about babies." I rolled my eyes. "So by the sound of things, you seem to be getting comfortable with the idea of keeping him if he's Bronte's son. Right?"

"No, not at all. It really all depends."

"On."

There was no way I was telling him that I thought I was pregnant and depending on that would likely add to determining my decision.

"I'm not comfortable with Bronte's mother taking him if I decided not to keep him anymore."

"What's wrong with his mother?"

"She only wants him for the check that she could collect."

"And you know this from?"

"People that know her. I want him to be with someone who is going to genuinely look out for his well-being. Not just because they see him as a paycheck."

"I still think the best place for him to be is right here with you. Who better than you to keep his father's memory alive?"

"Believe me, I used to think that too, until I had to care for him. It's hard, Cortez, especially alone. Not only that; a part of me is bitter. I hate to admit it, but it's true. It hurts like hell to know he has a child, and for it to be with Jackie... that's a hard pill to swallow. It's hard for me to get past that."

"As I said before, I think you don't give yourself enough credit. Golden, you're stronger than you think you are. I mean, you slept on a subway when the streets are brutal."

"But that's for me. I can do what I have to do for me, but him..."

"It's no different. I know he's not biologically yours, and maybe that's why you can easily let him go, since there's no connection, but you are legally married to his father. What do you think he'd want?"

"I get so angry at times I don't give a shit, because I feel like why should I care."

"Because you do, and I know you have a heart. Plus, you know that child is innocent."

"Why are you always lecturing me?"

"Somebody got to school you." He had me laughing

again. BJ was still up, just looking. "If you get his bathwater ready for me and his things together, I'll give him a bath now, since he needs changing."

"No!" He wasn't expecting that answer at all and narrowed his eyes at me, caught off guard. "Give me the baby. I want you to eat. I'll bathe him."

"Oh! Bet!" he said, pleased. "You don't have to tell me twice."

He gave me BJ, and I went and gave him a bath. When I got back, Cortez was in the kitchen just getting done cleaning it up and what Will had fixed. I never saw what it was. I just noticed it was gone. I had BJ all dressed in one of his new outfits. He was on my shoulder on his way to sleep.

"Wow! You cleaned up everything!" I eyed him. "Did you throw the food he cooked away?"

"I can if you want me too," he assured.

"Stop it!"

"Your plate is wrapped up in the fridge."

"Well I'm going to lay him down and then I'm going to get dressed."

"Alright! I see he has yet to get that crib put together. If you point me in the direction of some tools, I can handle that while you're getting dressed."

"Forget having things done for BJ. I can get used to this myself."

"So you say. I know you well enough not to take anything you say, in that regard, seriously."

I laughed. He was right. I played a lot when it came to Cortez. I would never allow myself to be serious with him. I knew it must've bothered him because he had always been serious when it came to me. Being this way was just easier. I showed him where the tools were and then laid the baby down. As I stared at him, I thought about Bronte. Cortez was right. I did care. I missed him. I missed him so much. I usually stopped myself from thinking about him because it made me angry, but staring at BJ, the tears just flowed.

He was the cutest little version of Bronte, but his skin was a shade lighter. He was like a smooth, buttery, chocolate tone. He had a head full of the biggest curls, and his eyes were a light shade of brown. He was so handsome. It just made me break down. Cortez came back after grabbing the tools he needed and saw me crying.

He set them down on the table and took me in his arms, allowing me to release all the hurt and pain I was feeling. He didn't say a word. He just closely held me. In that moment, it felt so good to be in a man's arms again. To be able to lay my head on a firm chest, even if it wasn't Bronte's. I felt comforted. I missed the smell of a man's scent around the house and other distinctions that made them men.

With my face drenched in tears, my eyes rolled up and met Cortez's. I knew what I was thinking was wrong, and what I was about to do was too, but I didn't care. His eyes blazed as he looked down into mine. With a lift of my chin, I crashed my lips into his, needing to feel loved. I held on to them like a leech, sucking for dear life. Cortez started kissing me back, but then he grabbed me by my shoulders and tore himself away.

"Gold... stop! You don't really want to do this."

Everything in me felt like I needed this. Doing what made sense never was the way I operated. Yes! I wanted to do this which was why I held on to him, staring with longing in my eyes, as they too begged to be satisfied.

"I do, Cortez. I know what I want. I really do! Please!"

"You're just grieving still, and I'm not going to take advantage of that."

My head shook frantically in disagreement.

"No! No! It's not taking advantage if it's what I want. Please, Cortez! I'm begging you." I got desperate and threatened him. "I'll... I'll just get what I want from Will if you won't give it to me."

Anger appeared in his eyes along with wrinkles in his nose as he clenched his jaws. His strong hands gripped my arms so tight as he stared at me and spoke in a firm but low tone.

"You think I don't want you? You think it's been easy for me to be around you and see you like this? I've wanted you since the day I've met you, but I respected your wishes because I respect you!"

I thrusted my arms back and yanked his hands away as I tried not to yell loud and wake the baby.

"I don't want your respect! I just want you! Just give me

what I want!"

"You really want me to do this?"

"Yes!"

I was more sure about that than anything. He gathered up the bottom of his t-shirt and pulled it over his head and threw it off. His sculpted arms and chest just slapped me in my face, as I stared at him. He continued to undress in front of me, and I couldn't take my eyes off him as he stripped. He did it so fast I was speechless and caught off guard at the same time. This man then stood before me in only his socks.

"Where you want it? Right here?"

"I uh... urm."

The blankets Will had were folded up on the couch. Cortez walked over and grabbed the quilt and spread it out on the open space on the floor, then stood on it. I quickly made my way to him and jumped up on him, wrapping my legs around him, madly kissing him.

I still had on my silk robe since I wasn't dressed yet. With one arm still around his neck, I used my free hand and undid my belt and wiggled my way out of one side and then did the same for the next as our lips were connected and he held me in his hands.

Now only in my panties, Cortez laid me down on the blanket. We continued kissing as he laid between my legs while his hands gently explored my body. His lips suddenly abandoned mine and traveled down to my girls and teased them with his tongue. I began grinding on him as I cuddled his face, anxiously waiting for him to take me there. He responded to my moans and removed my panties before inserting himself inside of me and stroking me nice and slow. His jewels were one of a kind. I had to remember how to handle his karats. Eventually, I had his dick on lock, trying to savor every ripple of it as his anaconda slithered and invaded me.

Every time we fucked, he made me squirt, and this time was no different. When I came, my body violently shook from the release. I had to watch my tongue because I didn't want to wake the baby for fear of not being able to get more. All I could do was pant like an animal. Cortez kept on going, and although I loved the invasion, my walls were getting beat the fuck down.

Had it been physically possible, his big ass would've been in my throat. That's how much he choked my uterus. The minute I started to get back with the program, Cortez was letting his load loose. I noticed there was a slight lag in him pulling out. Even though I knew it, I wasn't worried about it much.

A part of me figured I was possibly pregnant already, and also, I didn't have any condoms to even offer. If I wasn't pregnant, I hoped I'd still be okay. Cortez wasn't expecting to have sex with me anyway, so I knew he wasn't prepared. He just did as I commanded. Now I hoped none of this came back to bite us in the ass.

We went for another round, and then I hit the shower

while he watched the baby in case he woke up. Then he got in the bathroom. That bath had BJ knocked because he was still sleeping which was surprising. By the time Cortez came out the bathroom I had the blankets cleaned up and the living room back in order. I went in the kitchen to get something to drink. Cortez walked in there.

"Thanks for letting me borrow your shower."

"Sure! Hey! You still going to put the crib together for me?"

"Want me to put in even more work, huh?" he stated, shaking his head, smiling.

I smiled back.

"Well, it was your idea. I'm just asking, but if you're tired and all..."

He came close to me, heaving his big chest in my face.

"You know good and well it takes more than that to tire me out."

I put the tips of my left hand to his chest and pushed him back.

"The crib is waiting." His arms hung to his sides like the hulk as he stared at me. He chuckled to himself before walking out of the kitchen. "Would you care for something to drink?"

"Nah, I'm straight for now."

While he was putting the crib together, I got a text message from Will.

You still got company?

Yeah.

Tell him to leave. I wanna come back.

Lol! I wanna thank you again for taking care of me when I passed out and coming to my rescue last night.

I'm glad I was there to do it. How's the baby been? He handling that formula any better or the same?

Someone called Cortez's phone while he was doing the crib, breaking my attention from my phone. He answered it. I don't know why I was being nosy, but I listened to his end of the conversation to see if I could tell if it was a male or female on the other end. He looked in my direction briefly and when he did that, I went back to texting Will.

Not sure yet. He's been sleeping since I gave him a bath.

Oh dat's what's up!

I walked in the living room where Cortez was. Simultaneously, he was hanging up the call.

"You didn't have to hang up because I came in here."

His eyes roamed over to meet mine.

"I didn't."

"Oh," I said then curved my lips downward.

I let it go. It was his business and I had, nor wanted any part of it. As I watched Cortez put that crib up, I realized how quickly my life had changed. Then it dawned on me too, if BJ did have a problem with the formula, I had to find him a pediatrician. That thought alone had me shaking my head and heavily sighing.

"What's wrong?"

"Something else I just realized."

"Which is?"

"I have to find a pediatrician for BJ. What if he does have a problem with that formula? I'mma have to take him somewhere before the results come back."

"That's not a problem. I can get you a list of some in the area."

"That would really help. Thanks!"

"You know I'm always happy to help you," he said with a devilish grin.

"Anyway! So what you got planned for your next few days off?"

"I wanted to come and help you, but something did come up for tomorrow."

I waved him off.

"Don't worry about us. We'll be fine, and I can always call Will too."

Cortez frowned up his face.

"I'm sure."

"I'm not saying it like that. I just meant he's good with BJ, too, and doesn't mind helping me either. That's all."

"Where are you putting this thing?"

"In the bedroom. You put that together fairly quickly."

"I told you, I like to use my hands, and it also helps that I'm good with 'em."

I smiled as I remembered that conversation. While he rolled the crib to the room suddenly, I felt guilty for laughing and enjoying Cortez's company. Sometimes when I encountered an inkling of happiness, it made me feel bad that I allowed it. I figured I better follow him in there to tell him where I wanted it.

"I moved it right here since it seemed like a good spot."

He moved it along the wall near the walk-in closet. That actually was close to my side of the bed. It was perfect.

"Good choice!"

"Alright! What's next?"

"I would love to go out and get some fresh air, but BJ is still sleeping. Matter of fact, I'm going to go check on him because he's been out for longer than what I'm used to."

I walked in the room and peeked in on him and he was up but laying there quiet. I was struck dumb. Cortez was right behind me, so I looked over my shoulder at him.

"I wonder how long he's been up."

"I'll go get a bottle ready." He left the room.

As soon as I picked up the baby, my doorbell sounded. I didn't know who that could've been. With him in my arms, I walked over to answer it. It was Bronte's mother. I sized that ass up first as she stood on my porch. She crossed the line.

"What the fuck you doing here?"

"Since I didn't have your number, I came here to see my grandson." Cortez came over to the door and stood beside me.

"Is everything okay over here?"

"I got this!"

"Here, give me the baby while you two talk." Cortez took the baby from me and left us to talk. Bronte's mother looked at me with disgrace once he walked away.

"Your trifling ass couldn't even let my son's corpse get cold before you're on to the next one."

"Get the fuck off my property, or I'll have the officer you just disrespected have your ass locked up for trespassing."

"I'll leave for now, but I'm coming for my grandson. Mark my words," she threatened with a satisfying grin on her face.

With my hand in the air I gladly showed her my wedding ring.

"You have no right to him. And had you not been disrespectful to me from the beginning, I would've had no problem with you seeing him. But you left me no choice but to make it my mission to keep him away from you."

"You're not even fit to take care of yourself. There's no way you'll be able to care for him, and I'm going to prove that since you've made my case for me already, so watch ya back!"

"Lady, you don't want to fuck with me! I know the kind of mother you were to Bronte, so two can play that game." I leaned in a bit closer to her face. "You're no better than me when it comes to parenting, but the difference is, I won't screw this this little boy's life up like you did your son's. He moved you away because he didn't want to be around you!"

She had this haughty expression suddenly.

"Is that right? Is that what he told you?"

Cortez came back over and immediately started nudging

me away with his elbow.

"Okay, ladies, that's enough."

"Get off my property! Now!"

"You know, I was hesitant to say this. I was just going to let things play out, but since you want to get technical about things. My name is on the deed to this house. Not yours, nor my sons. So! You'll be receiving a sixty-day notice to vacate the premises. Consider this house up for sale. Have a nice day!"

That snobby yet ghetto bitch walked off the premises, proud of evicting her grandson. I was at a loss for words. I slowly shut the door and leaned my back against it. I didn't know what I was going to do. I had nothing! I couldn't believe Bronte got this house in her name. I wasn't prepared to hear that shit. Again, he lied to me. I was stunned and felt humiliated.

"You know what, I'm taking you out of here. You need some air." I was still stuck, paralyzed, by the door. He had BJ all bundled up and packed in his car seat. His baby bag was on his shoulder when he took me by the hand to leave. "Come on."

"Wait! I don't have my keys or my bag."

"The keys are sitting right here in his car seat. You don't need your bag. Let's go!"

"Go put him in the car. I'm coming. I promise. I just want to get my phone."

I grabbed that and my bag and got in Cortez's car. He

drove us to the beach. We parked down by it, in the lot where you got a picturesque view of the scenery. I got out the car and made sure BJ wasn't too hot since he was wrapped in his blanket. He was knocked out in his seat.

After that, I stood quietly on the side of the car with my arms folded and left with my thoughts. As the wind blew strands of my hair, I watched different ones as they enjoyed the water and the company of others. It made me wonder what their lives were like. Everyone seemed so happy.

I never understood why my life had to be so complicated. Nothing was ever easy. Nothing ever seemed to last, and nothing was more constant in my life than hurt and heartache. Two things I could always count on. For the first time in my life, I was afraid. Life was kicking my ass, and I felt like I was running out of the strength I needed to keep fighting.

"Hey." I glanced over to my left shoulder since Cortez's hands were on me. He was right behind me. A tear fell down my face. "You know everything is going to be alright, right?"

I wiped my face and spoke calmly.

"I don't know anything anymore."

"You know the offer still stands for you and BJ to come stay with me. I have plenty of room."

"It's not fair for me to interrupt your life like that, Cortez. I won't."

That made him walk in front of me. His hands cupped my elbows as his eyes zoomed in on mine.

"I want you there. Both of you."

"Cortez, it's something you don't know."

His eyes circled my face.

"What?"

I took a deep breath. I felt like I needed to lay all my cards out on the table with him. Then I second guessed myself and decided not to say anything since nothing had been confirmed.

"I'm a neat freak, and I like things kept a certain way. I can't tell you what to do in your own house, so my being there will never work."

He started laughing at me.

"You're making excuses, Golden. Besides, if she's serious about selling that house, where do you have in mind to go?"

"The only other person I could possibly turn to is Will."

I saw Cortez's jaws tighten at the mention of his name. He put his hands on his sides and turned away from me. I wasn't trying to be hurtful, but that was my other option and he asked.

"Well, my offer still stands, but you do what you want to do."

I knew for sure that made him upset. The truth of the matter was if I was pregnant with Bronte's baby, I didn't care about staying with Will, and him knowing. But I cared about me and BJ and then another baby burdening Cortez. He was too good for that. He still was too good for me. I couldn't put my problems on him any longer.

10

SEPTEMBER 1, 2006

Today I was finally going to the doctors for myself. These past few months had been strenuous, not leaving me the time to go, after I figured I waited long enough to see. Cortez helped me find a doctor's office for BJ and I finally had him checked out since he was still having issues. It was his formula like Will said giving him a problem, so with that change, he's been a new baby.

Bronte's mother also sent papers, as she stated, giving me a deadline to move, which was what I'd recently done. I didn't want to burden Cortez, nor did I want to live with Will, honestly, so I got over myself and called Kosha. This was my first time reaching out to her since she had been calling me, and it wasn't easy for me to ask her, considering how nasty I was toward her, but I did.

"Hello," she answered.

"Uh, hey!"

"Hey! I'm surprised you're actually returning my call."

"Yeah, Kosh, I gotta be honest with you..."

"Gold, I promise you, I am so sorry about what happened to Bronte and what I said to make us fight. You my home girl! I swear, I would've never said a word to him about Will. I just was pissed because I knew how much you loved Bronte, but I hated the way he treated you. I can't lie about that shit. Bottom line, it's your life, and I have to just say what I feel, when asked, and allow you to do you."

"I know. You don't have to apologize for caring about me. You've been my girl, and there for me through a lot of shit and again, I need you," I admitted with a crack in my voice.

"Bitch, what's wrong!"

"I... I found out that Bronte's mother owns this house, and she's selling it. Me and the baby have no place to go."

"Yes the fuck you do! You need me to come get y'all... what?"

I was silently crying on the other end of the phone. It meant a lot that she welcomed me back with no questions asked. I dried my eyes and blew out a breath first then resumed talking like I wasn't crying.

"No, I have my car. I still have to get the baby's things packed up and my clothes. Nothing else is mine, so once that's all taken care of, I'll give you a call."

"Aw I can't wait to see the baby and catch up."

"Yeah, we have a lot to catch up on."

"Alright! Well I have this girl sitting, waiting in my chair, so I better get back."

"Girl, you should've told me you were at the shop."

"It's fine. I told her it was an important call I had to take."

I smiled.

"Okay, I'll be in touch."

"Alright."

It turned out she made it easier than I deserved, but I was glad I asked. If things would've went the other way, then I would have asked Will, for sure.

We moved sooner than her sixty days. BJ and I left the minute I could get everything confirmed. From getting the results to the DNA test, which proved BJ was Bronte's son, to letting Jyreese know the deal as far as the bills, since I planned on packing up our belongings once I knew we could stay with Kosh. I didn't want to stay a second longer in her damn house.

His mother had been a total witch and still had plans of trying to take Bronte away from me. We actually had a hearing scheduled. I was not about to make that easy for her and knew I had to get my shit together. Not only for the possibility of court, but in case I was about to be a mother to two. Now that I had a moment, I was going to get this pregnancy finally confirmed, if that was my issue.

I stayed with the facility I found in *Arcchester*. The baby's doctor was here, and I didn't feel like looking for a new place back in *Iaburg*. The drive was like forty-five minutes to an hour away, depending on traffic. I didn't mind it. When I was finally seen, I heard some news that I had been expecting, but wasn't prepared for. I was pregnant.

I sat outside that office and covered my face, as I cried in my hands. Everything always had to hit hard. I hadn't even mentioned this to Kosha yet. I jumped when I felt an unexpecting hand on my shoulder.

"Miss, are you okay?"

My hands quickly cleaned my face off. I didn't know who this woman was, but I answered her.

"Yes, I'll be alright."

She then gave me a card. I looked at it and realized she was a counselor. Her name was Mrs. Katherine Waters.

"If you need to talk about anything, call me."

"Oh, no," I said as my head movement matched my mouth, "I don't... I can't afford to..."

"I work for a non-profit organization. Won't cost you a thing but your time, if you're willing to talk."

Her smile was warm, and there was something genuine about her as I stared into her face.

"Thank you."

After that, I figured I'd better get out of there before someone else tried to offer me something, considering how I looked. I must've had basket case written all over my face. Was I a wreck? Hell yeah! No hiding that, I guess. My mind was racing as I drove back to the house. I already was taking care of a four-month-old, and now this. Kosha had BJ for me since I told her I had something to do and couldn't bring him with me.

I did tell her about the baby not being mine, biologically. She was stunned. That really took her by surprise. Now I had to go in there and tell her that I was pregnant. Fuck my life! When I got in, Kosha was sitting in her spot on the couch. She stood on her feet all the time, so she made it a point to be off them at home. She was holding BJ. He was starting to stay up a little longer, which Kosha loved.

The funny thing was, I loved it too. We were finally starting to bond. He even started smiling, which just made my heart melt. I knew there was no way I could let him go. The first thing I did was sit beside Kosha and started talking to him.

"How's my munchkin! Huh! How's my munchie munch!" He blessed me with a crooked grin. I couldn't help myself and went in and kissed his soft cheeks. Then his little mouth opened, and he yawned. "Is somebody getting sleepy?"

"Yeah, he's been up for a minute. He's ate," Kosha said, touching his tummy, "he's been changed and just been chillin'."

I sighed heavily. Kosha knew something was up.

"What's wrong?"

"So much, but for starters, I found out that I was pregnant today."

"You fuckin' gotta be kidding."

"No, Kosh. I been suspected it, after Bronte was killed,

but I just was more afraid of it being true and having it confirmed."

"So are you not happy about it now that you know?"

"This pregnancy is hard to be happy about for several reasons."

"So, what are you going to do? Bitch, you know you about to have two babies the same damn age?"

"Believe me, I've thought about a lot of things. That was one of the reasons why I didn't think I should take care of BJ."

She grabbed BJ up, bringing his little body close to her breast.

"Biiitch, you ain't getting rid of my munchkin."

"I know that now, but it was all I could think to do. I really got to get my shit together. I hate having to be here with you and you having to deal with all my baggage."

"Yeah, you are going to need a hustle or something. You can't expect Bronte's boys to keep fronting you money, even though I know they all for it."

"No, I get you."

"Are you going to tell your two boy toys?" she said with laughter.

"Girl, please! Will and Cortez are not my boy toys. They've grown to care for BJ, and they also like looking out for me."

"And you don't mind," she gladly pointed out.

"I do, Kosh. I *really* do. I don't see them that often

anymore anyway, since I've been here, but I will tell them when the opportunity presents itself, I guess."

"Well, if I see anything or hear of any job openings, I'll let you know. I think Mela at the shop is looking for a shampoo girl. I think! But I'll double check."

"Oh no, Kosh! I'm already in your space at your house. I'm not going to be in your face at work too."

She got up to lay BJ down since he fell asleep.

"Suit yourself."

It intrigued me for a second, only because I did have a hearing coming up that, that witch was able to get the courts to grant. I definitely wanted to have something by then, belly and all. Fuck!

11

NOVEMBER 3, 2006

BJ's hearing was scheduled for today. Right now, it was just us that went before a mediator to hear each side. His mother came in there with a whole fur coat on, hair nicely curled. She wore a short cut, tapered on the sides. Bronte didn't look anything like his mother. I assumed he got his handsome looks from his dad.

She asked us both questions and I was proud to say that I was working. I got a job in a department store. I decided to call Mrs. Waters. I realized I needed to talk to someone who could possibly give me some good advice on this case. She gave me more than what I expected. She knew the hiring manager, and just like that, I was offered a job.

The pay wasn't shit, but it was a start. I'd worked before, doing cleaning jobs, and the minute I could get someone to be with BJ at night, I was going to find another job doing that. I was fortunate to get a daytime shift that would allow me to get him daycare thanks to Mrs. Waters. She was a light in my darkness. I was proud to be able to tell the moderator that and all the other support I had for BJ. I felt good once we came out of the room and Bronte's mother hated it.

"You really are pleased with yourself, aren't you?"

"Very!"

"I wouldn't be. The way you performed in there made you look like the ghetto trash you are. Taking handouts from every Tom, Dick, and Harry."

I shook my head in her face, unbothered.

"The mere fact that you have to say something to me let me know I did everything right in there. See, you thought that scene I made at a funeral was your ace in the hole, but you know what I have on my side that you don't? Love! For him! Not money!"

"This isn't over, so I wouldn't get too happy just yet. And for your information, you don't have a clue about what I love."

"Ahhh, think I got a pretty idea," I debated.

"I think I got an idea of what you love too, looking like ya knocked up already."

She walked away from me. If she wasn't his mother, I would've knocked dat ass out. I was mad number one, because of what she said, and two, I was tryna hide it from her judging ass. I knew Bronte was probably turning in his grave watching how we went at it. That woman was evil, and I was not going to let BJ be subjected to her miserable ass.

I put my coat on and proceeded out of the courthouse. On my way out, I bumped into Cortez. My eyes grew wide and the corners of my lips creased as I saw him.

"Well hello!"

"Hey!" He stopped in front of me. I thought I would've gotten a hug. "How'd it go today?"

"Honestly, I'm not sure. I want to say it went well, but we're still scheduled to come back. She wants to have full custody of BJ, and I don't want her nowhere near him."

"Who has the little guy anyway?"

"He's at daycare."

"Well, I just thought I'd see if I could catch you. I can't stay long."

"Oh! Yeah. Of course!" I tried not to show disappointment. I hadn't seen Cortez in a while. We'd spoken on the phone here and there, but it hasn't been easy since I'd been working and he was always working. "Back to work," I suggested.

"Yes and no. I do got some news to tell you too, so when's the next time you're going to be here in town?"

"Now! What is it?"

"I can't talk here, and plus I have to go. I'll call you!"

As he was walking away, I was heading to my car. Then my phone rang once I got outside, and it was Will. He and Cortez knew I had a hearing today, so the calls were expected. Although, I didn't expect to see Cortez and he be in a hurry like that. But Will wanted to take me to get something to eat. I was hungry, and since I didn't need to pick BJ up yet, I told him we could meet up.

It was freezing out that day too, so I knew I had to get BJ before nightfall when the temperature really dropped. Will said he was coming from his boy's house, whose wedding he was in, and told me to meet him at *The Cocoa Grill*. Will had gotten there before I did. He would have, since he was closer. I called him when I pulled up. He told me to give his name and they would seat me at his table.

This guy always had me somewhere fancy. Once I came in, the waitress led me right to him. He stood up and hugged me.

"How you doing today?"

"I'm okay."

His eyes sparkled as he looked at me.

"I feel like I haven't seen you in forever."

"Well it has been a few months. How's the job going?"

"Oh, work is great! I'm actually working on a new business venture with my boy."

I rubbed my hands on my legs as I smiled and admired his drive.

"You always seem to amaze me."

"Thanks, I guess," he said, smiling. We got our menus and ordered our drinks and food. "You are going to stay and eat this time, right?"

I laughed so hard.

"Shut up! Yes, I'm staying. I'm starving today."

"Good! So how's it going being back with ya home girl? Haven't had the chance to really talk to you much since the move. Y'all making out okay?"

"We're fine. My goal is to move, so I'm not in her space. Plus, I need my own."

"How's lil' man? I gotta come and see him. I know he's getting big."

"Yeah." I smiled as I thought about him. "He's staying up longer and showing more of his personality." I shook my head. "He's great!"

"I'm glad, 'cause you were going through it before, when he showed his personality."

"I'm not giving you no more props for the milk situation if that's what you're fishing for."

"Nah! Nooo," he toyed. "Had my man stomach in knots, but I'm glad he's doing much better."

"Who you telling."

"I'm sorry his grandma bugging and tryna take him from you."

"I never knew it would be like this with his mom. If I wasn't in that courthouse and she wasn't who she was, I would've got in her ass."

We got our food, and I dug right in.

"Gold, you got that baby now. You can't be acting like you

did when we were teenagers. It's time to put that behavior behind you."

I lifted my head from my plate and stared him in the eyes.

"What behavior?"

"You can't be just reacting without thinking about the consequences and who else ya actions affect, man. You got that baby," he cautioned while pointing at me. "If something happened to you, you could best believe grandma gon' happily takeover. She already tryna take him now. You can't afford to fuck up in *that* way."

I knew Will was right. He wasn't the only one who told me I needed to make some changes. Mrs. Waters knew some of my background, just some, but what she concluded after knowing how badly I needed a job, was that I had to always make sure I was thinking about what was best for BJ, if I continued to have him. She knew that was my whole reason for calling her, but she needed to know if it was out of sincerity or just because I didn't want his grandma to have him.

"You're right! It's going to take me some time to learn how to not be compulsive but for BJ's sake, I will do my best. I have to."

"Sounds like somebody's finally ready to be a grown up."

"Shut up, Will! I have something else I want you to know."

He put his fork down.

"What?"

"I just found out that I'm pregnant." He looked disappointed and shocked, but I had to tell him. I knew how Will felt about me, and I couldn't allow him to still have hopes of the two of us, when I knew that wasn't possible, especially now. "You've been so great to me and BJ, and I know I've said this to you already, but I just have a lot on my plate, and I really can't handle anything else."

"I had no idea you were in—"

"Wait! Before you say anything else, I had suspected this right after Bronte was killed. I've just been bombarded with so much I didn't have it confirmed until now."

"Wow!"

He was looking around the table like he was searching for some words.

"I'm sorry."

"For what? I mean, yeah, this news definitely surprised me, but Gold, you mean something to me. You should know a baby isn't going to change that. You don't want a relationship with me. I get that, but that's not why I've still been here. You're my friend. I care about you. I love you as a person and as a friend."

"But I thought you were only hanging around because you wanted something more. I thought you hoped I would change my mind if you stayed around me long enough. I thou—"

"Wrong! You thought wrong. Of course, I would love more, but you said no, and I have to respect it. That still doesn't change the fact that I'm going to still be here if you ever need me."

I started crying. Will came on my side of the booth and wrapped his arm around me.

"I've never had anyone care about me like this. At one point, you didn't."

"I know, and don't think I don't regret it, but now that I have you back in my life, my friendship isn't going anywhere."

I lifted my head off his shoulder and looked him in the eyes.

"I knew there was good in you, Will, which was why it hurt so bad when things ended the way they did."

"Well I can't change the past, but the future is a different thing."

"Some girl is going to be lucky to have you."

"I hope you know the same. That a man would be lucky to have you too, Gold. You're more than just sex, or someone's possession. A real man would know that. He'd never hit you either, or make you feel less than the prize that you are. But a coward will do what you allow. Don't allow anything less than the best from a man and yourself."

I smiled as more tears ran down my face. Who knew Will could be so insightful? I hugged him.

"Thank you for that." I let him go and wiped my face once more. "I better get going. I have to go pick the baby up."

"Let me come with you. I want to see him."

"Sure!"

Will followed me to the daycare and then to the house. He was so happy to see BJ. BJ was staring at him, likely wondering who was this face. It was so adorable because he gave Will a smile eventually, after talking to him. Once I got BJ down for bed, Will left. It had me thinking after he did leave. I'd never told Will about Bronte and I fighting, but it boggled my mind how he knew.

After Will left, I called Cortez back since I noticed he phoned.

"Hey! You busy?" I asked.

"I do only have a short period to talk, and what I had to say to you, I didn't want to over the phone, but now I have to."

"What is it, Cortez?"

"We found the guys that killed Bronte, Jackie, and Wayne."

"Oh my gosh! Really?"

"Yeah, I had more I wanted to talk to you about, but I'm about to go work on this case. I don't know how long I'll be on it, but I know for sure I won't be able to contact you."

"You're going undercover, aren't you?"

"If I can, I'll try to call you, but I just wanted you to know in case you called me and I'm not available. By no means am I ignoring you."

"Okay! Thanks for answering my question."

He laughed, knowing he didn't.

"I do hope everything works out with the case. I've always thought BJ should be with you."

"Yes, you have."

"Well, I got to go. I'll be in touch and Gold. Take care of yourself, okay?"

"... I will."

He hung up. I was so emotional and couldn't even explain why, but what was oh so clear to me, was out of the seven or eight years I'd been with Bronte, not once did I think about taking care of myself. Yes, my emotions could've been stemming from the pregnancy, or the fact that I was happy that justice was going to be served, but my emotions were less about Bronte and more about what Cortez said.

Cortez told me to take care of myself. Wow! I never thought about doing that in the context that I knew he was speaking of. Yeah, I did what I had to do to survive, but that wasn't the same as taking care of myself. It just dawned on me that I tend to get so wrapped up in other people and not enough into myself. I thought my whole world had gone when Bronte was killed, yet I'm still here.

The strange thing about all of this was, even though it had only been some months since Bronte's death, I hadn't had much time to sit and miss him, because I was too busy caring for his child and being hit with everything else that I discovered after his passing. And now that I did have a moment to think about the things that I missed about him, none of them seemed right anymore.

Those few words from Cortez resonated with me and hit so hard, especially after talking to Will tonight. It made me ask myself, did I ever love me? My parents didn't want me from day one. Since then, I'd spend so much energy loving others, but never taking the time to do it for myself. I cried because that was so eye opening. I owed it to myself to put just as much energy into me, as I did others. If I'd taken the time to do that more, I knew things would've been different with my relationships. That had to change. I really had to change, for the better.

TODAY WAS Thanksgiving and although this was one of those holidays, I never wanted to partake in, today I had no choice. Kosha was cooking and she made sure I helped. Which was fine. I said I needed to make some changes, and this was the start of it. I did my part Wednesday night because I was scheduled to work on Thanksgiving. The good part was I got off by dinner time so I could be there to spend it with her and her parent's.

By the time I came in, her mom was holding BJ and her dad was watching football on the television.

"Hello, Mr. and Mrs. Hall."

They both spoke to me. Then her mother started talking to me about BJ. He was so excited when he saw me. He had the cutest smile with his two teeth coming through. I picked him up and held him since he had his arms reaching for me. I kissed his cheeks several times and then gave him back to her mother, since I still needed to undress.

"He's been so good since I've been here." The moment I took off my coat her eyes went straight to my belly. "Baby, you pregnant?" she asked, looking like she'd never seen a pregnant person before. That led her father to look away from the TV at me. Then he went back to watching the game.

"Yes, ma'am."

"Aw, well congratulations!" Then she started talking to BJ. "You're going to be a big brother! You don't even know what that is, huh?" she said as she grinned.

I walked in the kitchen since I knew Kosha was in there.

"Girl, it smells so good up in here," I expressed as I was looking over her shoulder. She was putting some marshmallows on the sweet potato puff. I moved aside so she could put it in the oven.

"Once this is browned some we can eat!"

"I'm ready too."

"How was work? I bet that store was crazy today wasn't it."

"Girl, it's been crazy ever since the holidays were approaching. So… no one else is coming over here tonight?" I curiously inquired.

I sat down and got off my feet.

"Nope! You start inviting niggas over for holidays and shit, they start thinking they in. Speaking of holidays, have you started Christmas shopping for BJ? I have," she said happily.

"I hadn't even thought about it, honestly."

"Well, you need to. It'll be his first Christmas."

I rolled my eyes at her.

"Like he'll know anything about some damn toys."

"So! He don't need to know! You do! And don't give that I don't celebrate the holidays bullshit because you got kids now. Well, a kid for now, and it's not about you anymore. And let me remind you," she said, pointing in my direction. "It's your job to be better than your mother not just like her. I'm just saying."

My eyes popped wide open. She just said some real shit to me. I didn't want to be like my mother. In the beginning, I used to hate not celebrating the holidays. Going back to school and kids bragging about all the food they ate over Thanksgiving break, and the toys they had gotten over the Christmas holidays. I felt so left out. Then as I got older, I didn't care. I hated the holidays. I'd never want that for Bronte or this baby.

"You're right! I'm going shopping the next time I go to work."

Kosha looked at me like I was crazy.

"You serious? Just like that?"

"Yeah. You're right! I don't wanna be like my mother was. I'm getting him some toys for Christmas."

She hugged me so tight.

"Okay, let me check these marshmallows. They should be browned some by now."

They were. We had a good Thanksgiving. I had a lot to be thankful for and the biggest thing I was thankful about was not getting to spend a lot of time alone dwelling on Bronte's death. It hurt that he was killed. It also hurt that his son would never get to know him. If I had time to sit and just grieve, I didn't know what I would have done or where I'd be. I had felt dead inside, but BJ had forced me to keep going. He was a blessing for many reasons. He'd kept me alive and able to get to this point to start understanding love and for that I was truly grateful.

12

JANUARY 22, 2007

Christmas and New Year's Day had come and gone. Both were amazing because I allowed myself to enjoy them. I got BJ, some baby toys like an activity mat that he could lay and play on and also an activity support seat he could enjoy. Kosha got him the noisiest toys she could find. One being a piano activity seat. He loved banging and exploring on them all as he grew into them. We even took pictures with Santa.

I didn't do anything on New Year's Eve. I relaxed since I had the next day off. Kosha went partying like she usually did so it was just me and BJ, ringing in the new year. Even though he was sleeping, I had him right in my arms.

Today I was heading to the doctors for my prenatal appointment. Every time I drove back to this town, I thought about the life I had here with Bronte. It saddened me. It reminded me of what I never really had and what once meant everything to me that I lost. But since I was being lazy and didn't want to change anything, I brought this reminder on myself.

Luckily, these months had been flying by and if I was going to make any changes with anything it would be after I was finally stable living somewhere on my own. I was glad to know my pregnancy was progressing very well. I got emotional every time I heard my baby's heartbeat, which was a baby girl. Me having a daughter was going to be interesting, but I promised myself after talking to Kosha that I wouldn't be anything like my mother. Kosha was going to hold me accountable anyway like she nicely did about Christmas.

As I was headed out of the office I passed through the waiting area, and saw the television was on to a breaking news story. It was an update on a shooting that took place two days prior involving three undercovers and the suspect. My eyes were glued to that screen. When they showed the suspect, I was glad he had been taken to jail after he was treated for his injuries. Then when they showed the officers that got shot I nearly shit myself when I saw Cortez's face being one of them.

I heard them say they were recovering and named the hospital. That was all I heard. I left out of there as quickly as my waddling feet could take me. I was trying my best not to cry because they said the men were recovering which meant he wasn't dead. But that fear of not knowing his injuries, still ate at me as I traveled to see if I could visit. I could not bear to lose another person.

When I got to the hospital, they wouldn't let me see Cortez, no matter how much I begged, until I did what I should have all along.

"Look, please let me see him. We're not married, but I'm his baby momma. I've been out of town. He knew I was trying to get here. Please!"

The nurse folded her arms and stared at me with a careful eye.

"How come you didn't say that in the first place?" She mentioned with skepticism in her tone.

"I didn't think I had to."

"I'll be right back. You wait right here," she ordered. She still looked like she didn't believe me. I'm sure she went to his room. Fuck! I waited for a bit and then I saw her coming. "Follow me."

I took a deep breath and then followed. When I entered the room, he was sitting up in the bed with his foot bandaged and propped up. There was a woman coming up from kissing his cheek. I looked to the floor as I stood by the door not wanting to see any more or walk any further.

"I'll come back later," she said.

"I'll be fine."

I lifted my head and got a look at her face, the same time she looked at mine.

"Golden! Is that you!"

He did a double take before the corners of his mouth quirked up looking my way finally too.

"Ohhh, so that's why you said baby momma," I heard Cortez say, as I was looking at the female that I didn't recognize at first.

"Giselle, oh my goodness!"

She hugged me around my neck so tight.

"It's so good to see you! It's been so long!"

"Too long!"

"I gotta go." She looked at Cortez. "Give her my number." Then she stared back at me. "Congratulations on the baby. You had a sister tripping wondering who my brother got knocked up!"

We both started laughing.

"I know," I said, flinching as I walked toward him while she dashed out the door. "Please don't kill meee."

He lifted his arms out to me and I gave him a hug while he responded in my ear.

"I kinda would if I could move." I pulled back not surprised by his response. "I had no idea," he added as he stared at me with his detective hat now on.

"I'm sorry, but I don't want to talk about this yet," I said as I had my hand on my stomach.

"Please, have a seat," he encouraged as he looked at it.

"I can't believe that was Giselle. I haven't seen her in so long. She doesn't even look like she had a child."

"She's been a pain in my ass ever since I been in here," he complained.

"That's because she loves you. You were shot for heaven's sake. I would be fussing over you too. I mean, look at you. I'm relieved to come in here and see you sitting up and the only thing damaged on you is your foot."

"That's just because you can't see my heart."

My head dropped and my eyes went upward. He had me afraid.

"Cortez, what's wrong with your heart?"

"You just did a number on it coming in here pregnant. When did this happen and how come you didn't tell me? I've spoken with you many times and you said nothing... even saw you at the courthouse."

"Wait a minute. Are you mad at me?"

A quick flame leaped into his eyes.

"You know what? I am mad. I'm mad because for the life of me, I can't fucking stop myself from loving you, no matter how much shit you give me to deal with. Another baby," he announced as he looked away from me rattled, then focused back in on me. "Who's the father?"

"You are, Detective!"

"Nah, don't do that," he said, shaking his head looking downward.

I got out of the chair and sat my fat ass beside him on the bed.

"I was surprised at first too, believe me. Before we were

together, I realized that I hadn't had my period and suspected being pregnant. Since I wasn't sure of when I was on previously, I thought I'd give it some more time. But I, too, was thinking the baby was Bronte's."

"So how do you know that it's mine and not his? How do you know that?"

"From the date of conception. There's no way I'm carrying his baby, Cortez. He wasn't alive when I got pregnant. I wasn't pregnant when I thought I was. It turned out, then, I was only late because of stress, but then we had sex, and that's when I actually got pregnant." I put my hand on my stomach and looked down at it. "This is your baby girl. She's due in April."

"Wait... just wait a minute." I noticed his breathing was more erratic. He took a moment before continuing like he was doing the math in his head or because he was having a hard time believing it. "So that's our baby girl?"

I took his hand and put it on my stomach.

"She's yours. You're welcome to get a DNA test to confirm it after she gets here, but she's really yours, Cortez," I seriously said. "I would never lie to you about something like this."

As he held his hand on my belly stunned, with reluctance he tore his eyes away to look at me.

"Were you going to tell me?"

"I was. Not like this, but I was. By the time I saw a doctor and wrapped my own head around this pregnancy and the baby being yours, you were telling me that you were going on an assignment. Whenever I spoke to you again, I was going to tell you, but once I heard this, I had to come see you... make sure you were okay."

"Are you okay?"

I searched his eyes, not understanding.

"What does that mean?"

"You said you had to wrap your head around me being the father. How do you really feel about it? Were you hoping otherwise?"

"Cortez, I never was disappointed, if that's what you're wondering. My biggest fear was how you would feel about it and me also raising two babies alone... if everything works out with BJ."

He took me by the hand.

"You think I would let you raise my child alone?"

"I didn't know how you would take it, first of all. If this would be good news or you'd be upset."

"I could never be upset about sharing anything with you. I love you."

I swallowed hard as his piercing eyes laid into me. The corners of mine released a drop out of each one wetting my cheeks.

"Why do you say that to me? Why do you love me? I haven't done anything to deserve it."

"Because loving someone isn't something that has to be earned. Love is given freely, Golden, but you're so used to having to work for someone's attention and affections, that you don't understand that. You should never have to feel worthy of anyone's love. Don't you see that?"

"I don't deserve your love. You deserve so much better than me, Cortez. You always have."

"There you go. Haven't heard a word I said. Well how 'bout this... it's too late. I love you in spite of what you think I deserve or even yourself." He reached his hand out and stroked my tears with his thumb. "You just gave me another reason to love you even more. You know that?"

I squealed from trying to hold my cry in.

"You're always good to me. I never understood why."

"Let me ask you something," he said, taking his hand away. "Why do you love BJ?"

"Why?"

"Yeah, why?"

"I don't know! I can't just give you one reason why. I just do!"

"You just made my point for loving you."

I clasped my hands together and smiled. It really was that simple and easy to give love.

"Can I use your bathroom?"

"Go 'head."

I got up and went in there to use it. This baby had been sitting on my bladder. When I returned, a nurse was checking Cortez's bandages on his foot. I waited by the door until she was done before walking back over to him. She spoke to me and smiled as she was leaving.

"Are you in any pain?"

"No, they have me on hard meds, but I have a high pain tolerance anyway so... I didn't even realize I was hit until I saw a trail of blood." He stuck his hand out. "Come back over here."

I obliged and sat back next to him.

"You're going to be on crutches when you get out of here. Are you going to be able to manage?"

"I'll be fine... unless you want to come and take care of me," he alluded, smiling from ear to ear. "No, let me rephrase that. I want you to come stay with me so we can take care of each other and our baby."

I got antsy immediately and pulled away from him, since he had his hand over mine when I sat down.

"Cortez—"

"For real, Gold. I want you to live with me."

"Why?"

"What do you mean why? Mainly because I love you. You're having my baby. I want to be there for everything, and having you with me would mean everything."

"I—I just don't know how I feel about doing that. It's too soon. Plus, I have work to think about, and I'm just tired of not having anything to show for myself." I needed Cortez to really understand me. "If I come to stay with you, I'll be just doing what I've always done."

"I get your need to prove to yourself that you can do this on your own, but you're not on ya own. I'm here. I'm gonna be here for you, BJ, and our baby. Is it 'cause you're not sure about your feelings for me? If there *are* any." I was frozen as I looked at him. "Tell me, Gold. Believe me, I can handle it."

"When I saw your picture come up as one of the people that got shot, it scared me. It brought out so many emotions, and all I kept thinking was I couldn't take another death. I knew you were recovering, but I was still scared of what I didn't know. Then when I saw you, I was so relieved to see you up and the extent of what you endured. I do care about you Cortez, in a way I never thought I could." My eyes shifted toward my lap. "It scares me. You scare me." I raised my head and gave him direct eye contact. "Your love and kindness always have."

"Because it's real. Golden, you deserve so much more than what you've been exposed to. I want to give that to you. Show you how a real man treats a woman. Live with me, Golden. I know we can make this work."

I took a deep breath before I stood up.

"I have to go get BJ. I'll call you."

His lips curved inward as he shook his head and let the conversation go.

"Here, plug in Giselle's number." He said it to me, and I plugged it in my phone. I gave him a kiss on the lips. "Let me know you made it back, okay."

"Alright."

13

JANUARY 29, 2007

"Surprise!"

When Cortez came through the door of his home, on crutches, he was greeted there by his mom, Giselle, and me. His dad had picked him up from the hospital. His face had a bashful grin on it as he saw the "Welcome Home" banner, decorations, and I'm assuming, me. He had no idea I would be here.

Once his family got their hugs in, I went and got mine. He slouched down some so I could put my arms around his neck. Then I gave him a gentle peck on his lips.

"This is a nice surprise to come home to."

"Go on and sit down now," said his mom. "Doctor's orders."

He looked over at BJ, since Giselle had been holding him.

"What's up, man! Look how big he got." He took a few

steps closer to Giselle on his crutches. "Hey! You got teeth now and everything."

BJ started smiling at him. He turned into such a happy baby after he was put on the right formula. Cortez headed over to the couch, and his mom helped him prop his foot up on the ottoman. He wanted to hold BJ while he sat, so Giselle brought him over to him. We all socialized, and then later I helped his mom and sister cook dinner, although they wouldn't let me do much.

Once the evening winded down, his folks and sister left. We were in the living room, Cortez with his arm around me, just chilling watching TV, laughing about everything. BJ was sleeping in his portable crib that was brought here.

"Will I have the honor of your company tonight? I'd hate for you to leave now, with BJ."

"Oh! You don't know," I toyed.

"What?"

"We're here to stay if you'll have us."

His eyes twinkled, and he smiled so wide.

"What? You serious?"

"Well since you haven't been up the stairs, you can't see that our things are already here. Your sister and your dad helped me get my things here while you were in the hospital," I said proudly.

I could tell he was very excited.

"Are you sure?"

"I haven't been sure about a lot of things in a long time, but this I'm sure of."

He leaned in and gave me a sensual kiss.

"Your being here means everything to me."

"And believe it or not, your friendship and dedication has meant everything to me."

"I want you to know that even though I'm glad you're here, I won't push or have any expectations of you that you're not ready for. I know you've been through a lot, and I just want to assure you that I'm clear on how you feel. I've been waiting a long time for your heart, and when you give it to me... fully give it to me, I'll make sure you'll never regret it."

He was such a good man. I still felt like I didn't deserve him, but I was going to do everything I could to make sure I did.

"Thank you for saying that, even though it wasn't necessary. I know you're a man of your word. I know that. You have always been good to me. Loved me like no other and have always wanted what was best for BJ, a child you also have no connection to. There is no doubt that I won't regret being with you. I also know you're going to be a wonderful father to our baby girl."

He looked toward my belly and put his hands on it while smiling.

"I still can't believe this is real. I'm going to make you so happy."

"I hope to do the same."

APRIL 15TH, 2007, our daughter Samara came screaming into this world. I knew right away she was going to be a firecracker. We couldn't have been any happier. BJ seemed to be adjusting to another little person besides himself in the house, which made us so happy. Even though he was still young it was important to Cortez and me that he still felt like he was loved like he was our only baby.

Back in February, me and Bronte's mom were scheduled to go to court, but she never showed up, so the judge granted me full custody. I didn't know why she wasn't there nor did I care, but I was so overjoyed, I cried. I was hormonal too, but that ruling did make me so happy. I'd been nothing but happy since I'd moved in with Cortez. I had never felt this loved, wanted, and appreciated in my life!

I was with a man that did what he said and was truly committed to me and our children. He treated me with the utmost respect and provided all our needs. I'd never experienced anything like this before, it still felt surreal. I am glad I was finally open to him, and what he had to offer. He loved me unconditionally, through all my mess and baggage and showed me what love was. I'm grateful to him.

I'm also thankful that Kosha kicked me out, a second time. She meant well. She knew Cortez had what I needed. Now I do. I hold myself to a higher standard because of him. I'm learning to love me more because I don't want to give him anything less. I know now not only do I deserve it, but he deserves the best of me, because he has always given me the best of him.

This girl's eyes are open. I could finally say goodbye to that broken-hearted girl, that never knew what love felt like and hello to making room for a heart to receive love, that I never knew existed... real love! And it feels Golden!

*PSA Domestic violence of any kind is not okay. Do not let anyone convince you otherwise or make you feel like their violence is deserved. If you or anyone you know is experiencing Domestic violence please know that there is help. Call the National Domestic Hotline at 1-800-799-7233 or TTY 1-800-787-3224. Get help. Get out.

The End

PLEASE JOIN MY READING GROUP!

CPSIA information can be obtained
at www.ICGtesting.com
Printed in the USA
LVHW041533081020
668326LV00013B/1175